Manuel Vázquez Montalbán was born in Barcelona in 1939. Joining the Spanish Communist party in his student days, at the age of twenty-three he was imprisoned for four years by a military tribunal for supporting a miners' strike. He started his career by writing satirical articles for a left-wing magazine in the last years of Francoist Spain and then went on to become a respected poet and novelist. Renowned for creating Pepe Carvalho, the fast-living, gourmet private detective, Montalbán won both the Raymond Chandler Prize and the French Grand Prix of Detective Fiction for his thrillers, which are translated into all major languages. He died in October 2003.

Also by Manuel Vázquez Montalbán and published by Serpent's Tail are *Murder in the Central Committee, Southern Seas, Off Side, An Olympic Death, The Angst-Ridden Executive, The Buenos Aires Quintet* and *The Man of My Life*.

Praise for Manuel Vázquez Montalbán

'Montalbán writes with authority and compassion – a Le Carré-like sorrow' *Publishers Weekly*

'Montalbán is a writer who is caustic about the powerful and tender towards the oppressed' *TLS*

'A love of fine food and murder combines in the adventures of Pepe Carvalho, who not only happens to be a private detective with a CIA past and Communist party contacts but a gourmet cook to boot. And Barcelona positively vibrates through these books' *Evening Herald*

'The attractively sceptical Carvalho simmers up gourmet meals and meets his share of dames, thugs and quislings, while trying to tug secrets from a city still scared of its memories' *Guardian*

'If you haven't yet made the acquaintance of Carvalho now's the time. He's the most original detective to come along in an age and the mix of political intrigue, Barcelona style, and Catalan cooking tips, makes for a great read' *Venue*

'One of the most engaging heroes to have graced a crime novel... the story is taut and the characters are irresistible...while the background throws light on many aspects of contemporary Spain, from the seedy underbelly to the indiscreet charms of the bourgeoisie' *Sunday Times*

'An inventive and sexy writer...warmly recommended' *Irish Independent*

'The most metaphysical gumshoe on the streets...the plot is as concerned with exploring capitalism's malignancy as it is with corpses and femmes fatales' *The Times*

'With Carvalho's love of fine living, and his always sympathetic eye for the virtues and resilience of the poor, Montalbán manages to make an essentially bleak world view feel almost optimistic. This is nothing less than world-class crime fiction, packed with three-dimensional characters, honest appraisals of the contemporary world and vivid writing. That you'll want to know what happens next comes almost as a bonus' *Big Issue in the North*

'His philosophical discussions, laced with cynicism and humour, climax at a dinner party which is sheer, murderous farce' *Sunday Telegraph*

'Artists, scientists, politicians, psychiatrists, cooks, and boxers all mingle in prizewinning author Montalbán's rich and convoluted novel...Montalbán's writing about food alone would make this book well worth reading' *Good Book Guide*

Tattoo

Manuel Vázquez Montalbán

Translated by Nick Caistor

A complete catalogue record for this book can be
obtained from the British Library on request

The right of Manuel Vázquez Montalbán to be identified
as the author of this work has been asserted in accordance
with the Copyright, Designs and Patents Act 1988

First published in Spain as *Tartuaje* in 1976

First published in this translation in 2008 by Serpent's Tail,
an imprint of Profile Books Ltd
3a Exmouth House
Pine Street
London EC1R 0JH
website: www.serpentstail.com

ISBN 978 184668 667 2

Typeset at Neuadd Bwll, Llanwrtyd Wells

Printed by Printed in Great Britain by CPI Bookmarque,
Croydon, CRO 4TD

10 9 8 7 6 5 4 3 2 1

This book is printed on FSC certified paper

Bold and blond as beer was he
A heart tattooed on his chest
Yet his sad voice was filled
With a song that was yearning for rest.

'Tattoo'
Song by Rafael de León

The golden girl had dived off the pedalo. The olive-skinned bald man swam as fast as he could to get a closer view of her returning to the surface, to glimpse her wet body streaming with water in the bright sunlight. The noonday heat was scorching the shore. The bald man swung his legs down, realised he was not out of his depth, and tried to spot where his family was on the beach. A cube of a woman was busy washing a child. The man continued scanning the beach, saw he was in no danger, and turned back to get a good look at the golden girl. By now she was swimming on her back away from the stationary pedalo, which was rocking gently in the calm sea.

That was when he saw the body floating in the water, a bobbing presence like the pedalo. It must be the golden girl's companion, who he had not noticed before. But that did not mean he wasn't allowed to look at her. Nobody could stop him gazing, filling his eyes with that solid flesh vivified by the salt and lustrous brightness. His gaze alternated between her as she swam strange bursts through the water and the body still floating obstinately alongside the pedalo. It slowly dawned on him that its position was too emphatic, and contrary to the laws of breathing. But some people can hold their breath for ages, he told himself, and I'm not going to be the fool who shouts for help and then finds the guy is as right as rain and has the girl laugh in his face. Now she was swimming the crawl back towards the pedalo, in an easy straight line, as though in her own lane in the sea. She stopped a yard from the pedalo and stared, first suspiciously and then with growing alarm, at the body, which just went on bobbing up and down as the waves pushed at it. The girl looked round to see whether anyone else had noticed; her eyes alighted on the bald, olive-skinned man, who was no more than twenty yards away. Reassured by his presence, she swam closer to the body. When she reached out and touched it, the strange swimmer floated away from the pedalo as obediently as a dead dog. The girl turned to look at the snooper and shouted something in a language he did not understand. He waited no longer. He tried to swim with great style to arrive looking cool and composed alongside this wonderful girl. But the sight of the lifeless corpse won out over his appreciation of her beauty. The bald, olive-skinned man pushed the body to shallower water where he could stand, then dragged it towards the shore. Still screaming, the girl followed him. The noise burrowed its way between those who were swimming and those distilling or drying sweat on the sand. Several swimmers tried to steal the starring role from the bald, olive-skinned man, but he clutched his prize firmly, with one arm looped under the corpse's shoulders.

When he reached the water's edge, four of the onlookers hauled the body out. The bald, olive-skinned man directed operations. They carried it face down, just as it had been pulled from the sea. He was wearing only a pair of trunks. He was young and blond, his whole body suntanned. The four bearers turned him on to his back on the sand. A cry of horror expanded the circle of the half-naked crowd. The body had no face. Fishes had eaten his cheeks and eyes. They quickly turned him over again. It was then that a little kid noticed there was a tattoo on his back. A hand brushed away the wet sand. Somebody read out the motto tattooed on his shoulder-blade: BORN TO RAISE HELL IN HELL.

It could only be the doorbell. Pepe Carvalho's hand groped for the alarm clock, but the heart of this nervous animal was not beating loudly. Someone was at the door. He tapped Charo's naked shoulder where it protruded from the sheets.

'There's someone at the door.'

'Go and open it, then.'

'It's your flat. How should I know who it might be?'

'What time is it?'

By now Charo was almost awake, and seemed keen to know what was going on.

'One o'clock.'

'At night?'

Pepe Carvalho pointed to the shafts of sunlight pouring through the shutters on to the bedroom floor. Charo leapt out of bed. Her naked body quivered; she wrapped it in an embroidered silk dressing gown. She put on her slippers, tidied her unkempt hair, and left the room. Raised on one elbow, Carvalho listened to the typical sounds of a door opening, followed by a short conversation, then the door shutting again. The slippers came slapping back across the wooden floor. Charo looked annoyed and disappointed.

'Fat Nuria.'

'Who?'

'Fat Nuria. The apprentice at Queta's hairdresser's. It's you she's looking for. Her boss wants to see you.'

'Why? How did she know I was here?'

'What kind of a neighbourhood do you think I live in? You can send her packing if you're not interested.'

But Pepe had already left the bedroom. He found himself face to face with a fat adolescent. Her rotund attractions could not hide the look of sly malice in her eyes. They surveyed Carvalho's only half-hidden bulk with an air of fellow-feeling.

'The boss would like to see you.'

'Who is your boss?'

'Señor Ramón, Señora Queta's husband.'

'What does he want?'

'He says you're to come. He says it's urgent. Here, take this.'

She held out a piece of paper. Carvalho pushed open a shutter so that he could read it properly. 'I've got something that might interest you.' Carvalho dropped the note on to the hall table and went back into the bedroom. His clothes were draped all over a rocking chair. He sorted them out and put them on; Charo meanwhile was busy with her blackheads at the dressing-table mirror.

'I'll be back tomorrow. Are you very busy today?'

'Four or five of them, from seven onwards.'

'They all quiet sorts?'

'Hmm... a bit of everything. But you can come to spend the night if you like.'

'I have to go home, to see if there are any letters. I've let things get into a bit of a mess.'

Carvalho headed off back towards the hall, then changed his mind and aimed for the kitchen instead. The fridge was as empty as it was brightly lit. He stuck a finger in the cream on a dish of Lyonnaise potatoes, then licked it. He decided to drink some chilled water and eat half a slab of chocolate. He saw there was still some champagne in the bottle that Charo always kept in her fridge. He uncorked it and drank a little of the freezing, flat but welcome liquid. He poured the rest down the sink, but as he turned round, he saw Charo standing in the doorway. Her face was covered in cream, and she was wearing a white dressing gown.

'Thanks for emptying it for me.'

'It was flat.'

'I like it flat.'

'Sorry.'

By then Charo had already disappeared from the doorway, leaving the way clear for him. He went back into the hall, where Fat Nuria was puffing and blowing impatiently. In the lift he gazed out of the corner of his eye at the adolescent's fluffy mountains of flesh; she accepted his appraisal through half-closed lids. Carvalho let her get out of the lift first, then followed her along the pavement. Fat Nuria walked along like a starlet, trying to flick her short, over-lacquered curls into the air. The city was entering its midday period of truce; the air was filled with the creaking sound of metal shutters being wound down for the end of morning business. They walked through cavernous streets of run-down buildings until they came to Calle de la Cadena. Fat Nuria speeded up and Carvalho soon saw the sign for Queta's hair salon. Beyond the frosted-glass windows he was greeted by the spectacle of a few remaining clients under hairdryers, their faces distorted by the plastic bubbles and with white towels wrapped round their necks. Carvalho studied the hairdressers' legs. They all seemed to be wearing red plastic slippers. One especially pert backside beneath a blue overall caught his eye.

'Who's that fourth one?'

'That fourth what?'

'The hairdresser at the back of the room.'

'That's Queta,' said Fat Nuria without looking round as she climbed the wooden stairs up to a small office bathed in neon light. Behind a pre-war office desk, a man raised his head when he saw them come in. He made the most of the sparse hair that grew round the sides of his head, while his white, freckled face allowed a few wrinkles to betray his age. He was wearing a grey suit, with a pair of leather slippers on his feet under the desk.

Fat Nuria left as soon as the man at the desk and Carvalho had acknowledged each other's presence with a stare. Carvalho accepted the other's silent invitation and sat in a narrow green plastic armchair. The man did not look the type to be in a business like this, or to be wearing slippers. Carvalho could sense that he was being studied, weighed up, assessed. The man finished his examination and looked away as though searching for something on the desk. It was a newspaper cutting, which he handed to Carvalho. The detective read it, and kept it between his fingers, but said nothing and went on staring at his host's peculiar complexion.

'Did you hear about it?'

'No.'

'Don't you read the news?'

'Sometimes.'

'What do you make of it?'

'What about you?'

'I asked first.'

Carvalho shrugged. The other man had leaned back in his wooden swivel chair and seemed content to await developments. Carvalho took his time, studying this small office in a small local business, similar to any small office in any small local business. The only thing out of place was this elegant, well-preserved man sitting opposite him.

'I'm interested to know who this man is, and what he did in life.'

Carvalho looked down at the press cutting.

'I don't think that would be too difficult. The police must have identified him by now.'

'I'm not interested in asking the police.'

'That would be the quickest, cheapest and most reliable way.'

'I'm not interested in how quick or cheap it might be. And everybody has their own idea about what might be reliable. I prefer not to lie to you, which is why I prefer not to tell you why I'm interested in finding out who that man is.'

'Perhaps you're interested in collecting stories about drowned men. This one is quite interesting. You don't see a tattoo like that every day of the week.'

'If you need to know motives in order to get on the case, make them up for yourself. I want to know the identity of that body.'

'I need something to get started with. The cops take this kind of thing seriously, and if I stumble around blindly I'm bound to trip over them.'

'I've heard very good things about you.'

'I'm sure you have.'

Carvalho let the cutting fall on to the paper-strewn desk, and resumed his silent contemplation of the other man.

'You know who I am. My name is Ramón, and I run this business with my wife. Let's just say it's aroused my curiosity, and I don't mind spending money on a whim. I want to know who that man was. All we have to go on is that from the description he was a young man, and he had that tattoo.'

'Have you nothing else to say to me?'

'Yes. I'll pay you a hundred thousand pesetas.'

'Plus expenses.'

'So long as they're reasonable.'

Carvalho was already on his feet. The other man had also stood up for the first time, and was leaning his weight on his hands. Carvalho saw he was wearing a huge gold signet ring in the shape of a Native American chieftain's head.

'Fifty thousand up front.'

No sooner had the word 'fifty' left his mouth than the man's hand skulking behind the Native American chief delved into a wooden drawer and pulled out a bundle of notes. He counted out thousand-peseta notes until he reached fifty, then pushed them across the desk at Carvalho.

The detective stuffed them in his pocket and went back to the staircase. His feet brought out the music of the wooden steps, and when he reached the salon he looked round for the same backside that had impressed him so much on the way up. This time, however, Queta was facing him: the round, pleasant face of a woman of about forty, perhaps a little too much make-up, the eyes a little too large.

By the time he was out in the street again, Carvalho was thinking he had missed an opportunity. Señor Ramón had given him fifty thousand, but there were at least another fifty still in the desk drawer. Which meant he had been prepared to pay him the whole lot there and then.

The restaurant smelled of kidneys cooked in sherry. Carvalho went over to a corner table from where he could survey the whole room, and allowed the smell to invade his nostrils, mouth and tongue. He ordered a 'Castilian salad' and the kidneys. He tried to imagine what on earth the adjective 'Castilian' might mean when coupled with the noun 'salad'. His imagination was far greater than the chef's. It turned out to be no more than chunks of marinaded tuna strategically placed on top of squares of soggy potato.

Concentrating on the scarce chunks of tuna, Carvalho also had time to scan the restaurant tables. He soon sized up the place and its customers. He asked the waiter:

'Is Bromuro around?'

'He's just finishing with a client down below. If you like, I'll tell him to come over.'

'Yes, do that.'

Bromuro arrived just as Carvalho was mopping up the kidney sauce with his bread. He was contemplating the chunk of bread smothered in brown gravy and then offering it to his expectant palate. A plate of kidneys is above all a pleasure for the senses of smell and touch, and Carvalho did not allow Bromuro's arrival to spoil his enjoyment. Bromuro knelt down beside him, then lifted one of Carvalho's feet on to his bootblack's box.

'Are you here to eat or to work?'

'Both. The body of a dead man has been found on the beach. He had no face. It was eaten away by the fishes. But he did have a tattoo on his back: *Born to raise hell in hell.*'

'Some people have all the luck.'

'You said it.'

'And was his sad voice filled with a yearning for rest?'

'What the fuck are you talking about?'

The shoeshine's watery eyes sank still farther into the network of black lines that made up a face that was half wrinkles, half purple veins. He was laughing, or at least that was how Carvalho interpreted the seismic convulsion of the wrinkled mass down by his knees.

'It's an old song. It was called "Tattoo". Concha Piquer used to sing it.'

All at once, Carvalho remembered it too. With Bromuro's help, he started to hum it, uncertainly at first, but then with more emphasis. The shoeshine sang it as though it were flamenco, but in fact it was a waltz. Carvalho let him get on with it. When he had finished, he bent down as if he wanted to see the results of the work on his shoes.

'I need anything you can find out about this.'

'For the moment I haven't heard a thing. Nada.'

'But now you know I'm interested. Tomorrow at one I'll be in the Versalles to have my shoes cleaned again.'

'Are you going whoring?'

Carvalho gave him an ambivalent smile and lifted his

other foot. Through the few remaining strands of hair, he could see the flakes of dandruff on Bromuro's skull. The shoeshine made his living as an informer, selling pornographic packs of cards or ingratiating himself by telling stories about how the occult powers used and abused bromides.

'I tell you, they put bromide in everything we swallow, just so that we won't go crazy, so that women can walk in the street without fear. It makes me feel so bad! So bad! So many women and so little to satisfy them with!'

Bromuro knew he was on to a sure thing with his talk of the bromide conspiracies and the distance between reality and desire. He had been entertaining the locals with his story for twenty years. He had started out using it as an example of his erudition, of how he knew all about the scientific progress of humanity. Then one day he discovered that people found what he was saying more amusing than troubling, and so he turned it into one of his main sources of tips. On this occasion, Carvalho slipped five hundred pesetas into the bootblack's waistcoat pocket. Bromuro lifted his head to show his surprise.

'Lots of dough involved?'

'Enough.'

'You don't usually hand out five hundred pesetas like they were a glass of water.'

'If you think it's too much, you can give it back.'

'No, I'll see you tomorrow, OK, Pepe?'

He picked up his box and walked away down the central passageway of the restaurant, peering to left and right at the customers' feet as though he were mushroom hunting.

Carvalho left the money for the meal on the saucer and went out. He could not immediately remember where he had left the car the night before, but felt intuitively it must have been farther up the Rambla. He walked up the centre of the avenue, stopping here and there at newspaper kiosks and bookstalls, picking up envelopes with plant seeds in them, wondering about the fate of the birds and small monkeys in their cages. The Rambla was quickly filling up with afternoon crowds, so Carvalho made his way under the hanging sign at the entrance to the Boqueria Market. He wanted to eat well that night. He needed to be cooking while he mulled over the problem of the dead body in the solitude of his own home, and knew that the best way to end the day was with a good meal. He bought fresh monkfish and hake, a handful of clams and mussels, a few prawns. The white, treasure-filled plastic bags dangled from his hands as the market came to life again for the afternoon. A lot of the stalls were shut, and buying food this late in the day made it feel as though he were entering a different time zone, a strange ambience filled with almost total silence, disturbed only by the sounds of buying and selling.

Strolling aimlessly around the market was one of the few ways that this tall, dark-haired man in his thirties, who somehow contrived to look slightly dishevelled despite wearing expensive suits from tailors in the smartest part of town, allowed himself some spiritual relaxation whenever he left Charo's neighbourhood and headed back to his lair on the slopes of the mountain overlooking Barcelona.

To reach Carvalho's house you had to go up along a wide dirt road that wound between old, over-ornate villas, their white walls stained grey by the rain of fifty years. The house fronts were brightened up by a scattering of green or blue tiles; clumps of bougainvillea or morning glory hung over their garden fences. Carvalho's villa was not of the same pedigree. It had not been built when Vallvidrera was in its heyday, but during its second wave of popularity, when some of those who had made fortunes on the black market after the war had retired to the mountainside for the splendid view it gave them of the scene of their splendid achievements. They were small-time crooks who had got rich through small-time black-marketeering. People who saved their money and who still had the pre-war nostalgia for a house and garden in the suburbs, if possible with a vegetable patch for their lettuces, potatoes and tomatoes, fascinating hobbies for those with free weekends and paid holidays.

Carvalho had rented a small villa built vaguely in the modernist style popular in the 1930s. The architects had obviously designed a starkly functional building, but the client must have wanted 'a bit more colour', or 'something to soften it', so they had allowed him a few courses of red bricks up on the cornices which looked like the gaps between teeth, and stuck some yellow tiles on the front, which had once been ochre but now after thirty years had turned green.

Carvalho took the mail out of the box and walked across the bare garden with its loose paving stones that led up to the front door steps. Carvalho's neglect had allowed weeds to sprout everywhere, and on the porch rotten leaves from the previous autumn had formed a slippery light brown mulch that shoes invariably brought into the house. Carvalho's feet trod their way across the geometric tiles of the entrance hall, and followed the trail of light his hand magically produced from the switches. July filled the evening sky with warmth, but Carvalho needed to light a fire if he was to think in a relaxed mood. To compensate, he stripped off to the waist and opened shutters and windows to allow the drier outside air and the last sunlight into the house. As he pushed open the shutters, his eyes took in the green horizons to the north and east, as well as the urban geometry of the city laid out at the foot of the mountain. Today the cloud of pollution was reduced to a kind of polar ice cap hanging over the industrial, working-class districts by the port.

Carvalho went to the basement to fetch firewood. He made several trips, and then had to clear out the remains of the fire from five days earlier. Four nights at Charo's were too many. Carvalho was in two minds. On the one hand, he felt bad about abandoning his own home and a regular, more routine existence. On the other, he remembered Charo's velvet skin, and the softness of her more intimate recesses. She had even caressed him tenderly.

He searched in vain for some newspaper to help light the pile of firewood he had built according to the how to book of good fires. From bottom to top, the wood formed a strict pyramid from smallest to heaviest. But he had no paper to start it with.

'I should read the news more often,' he said out loud to himself.

In the end he had to go over to one of the bookshelves that lined the room. He hesitated, but finally chose a big green book with lots of pages. As he carried it to the funeral pyre, Carvalho read some fragments at random. It was entitled *Spain as a Problem*, written by someone called Laín Entralgo at a time when it was thought that Spain's problems consisted simply of the problem of Spain itself. He pushed the open book under the sticks in the fireplace. As he lit it, he again felt torn: on the one hand, he did not like to see the book burn; on the other, he could hardly wait for the flames to shoot up and reduce it to a pile of obliterated words.

Once the fire was burning brightly and warmly, Carvalho went to the kitchen and laid out everything he had bought in the order he would need to cook them. The first thing was to go down to his wine cellar. He had had the partition between two walls knocked down, which left the soil and rock of the mountainside exposed. In the gap he had dug a small cave, where the dusty sides of wine bottles gleamed dully by the light of an infrared bulb. Carvalho looked along the row of whites, and eventually chose a Fefiñanes that was one of the few Spanish wines in his selection. Clutching the Fefiñanes in one hand, he was tempted by a Blanc de Blancs from Bordeaux. But his dinner was not worthy of this French wine. Each time he came down to his cellar, he carefully picked up and looked at one of the three bottles of Sauternes that he was storing for his Christmas seafood feast. Sauternes were his favourite white wine, apart from the incomparable Pouilly-Fuissé, which in his opinion ought to be reserved exclusively for the last wishes of intelligent gourmets at the end of their tether. He sighed, still clutching his Fefiñanes, and climbed back up to the kitchen. He cleaned the fish and peeled the prawns, then boiled the fish bones and the pink shells together with an onion, a tomato, some cloves of garlic, a hot pepper and strips of celery and leek. This liquid was essential for Carvalho's *caldeirada*. While he was gently bringing it to the boil, he fried some tomato, onion and more peppers. As soon as the mixture started to thicken, he poured it over some potatoes. Then in a pot he placed first the prawns, then the monkfish and finally the hake. The fish took on colour and added their juices to the mixture. Then Carvalho poured in a cup of the strong fish broth. Ten minutes later, the *caldeirada* was done.

Carvalho laid the table in front of the fire and ate straight from the pot. The chilled Fefiñanes, though, had to be drunk from a tall, elegant wineglass. To each wine its own glass. Carvalho did not usually follow style diktats, but this was one he strictly adhered to.

After his meal he drank a cup of the weak American coffee he had dicovered in San Francisco, and lit up a Montecristo No. 1. He sprawled across two sofas so that he could get completely horizontal, and lay with cigar in one hand and coffee in the other, gazing dreamily at the flames wavering as they disappeared into the sooty heights of the chimney. He was imagining the body of a young, blond man, 'bold and blond as beer', according to the song. A man capable of having that motto tattooed on his back: *Born to raise hell in hell.* Among the stories about tattoos he could recall, one stood out: Madriles, the poor crook who had put *Death to all cops* on his chest. He had paid dearly for this open declaration of principles, spending almost thirty years in jail alternately for petty crimes and for being a vagrant. Looking at El Madriles' tattoo had become a favourite pastime in every police station in Spain.

'Come on, Madriles, let's have a look at it.'

'I swear it was nothing more than a mistake, Inspector, sir. I was drunk when it occurred to me. The maestro who tattooed me warned me at the time: Madriles, it'll only bring you trouble.'

'So another spot of bother won't matter much. Go on, Madriles, take your shirt off.'

The tattooist. Somebody must have given the young man 'as bold and blond as beer' that tattoo. There weren't many experts left, but this was a professional tattoo, the sort young girls went in for when they wanted to leave a mark on their flesh and in their minds. This one must have been done by a professional. If not, the same water that had given the fishes the time they needed to gorge themselves on the dead man's face would have washed away the motto by now, and the body would have emerged from the sea not only stripped bare by death, but rendered completely anonymous – unless his fingerprints were in police records somewhere. His ID card, thought Carvalho. Of course they would be in the police records. He pondered on a possible link between the dead man and his client. There must be some connection between them. Carvalho tried to brush aside this hypothesis. He knew from experience that the worst thing to do in any investigation was to start from a hypothesis. That can only restrict the approach to the truth, and sometimes even distort it.

By the time he had finished his first litre of coffee for the night, the fire was crackling loudly and had turned the entire room into the backdrop for its wild but fettered dancing. Carvalho was hot; he stripped to his underpants. This lasted only a moment, just long enough for him to identify his own white body with that of the corpse: he shuddered, and rushed to get the protection of a second skin, his pyjama jacket.

He woke when he was tired of sleeping. Through the shutters of the half-open window he could hear the birds chattering among themselves about how bright and hot the day was. He looked out of the window and saw that everything was where it ought to be: the sky was up, the earth down. The electric heater and the Italian coffee-making machine helped him recover a sense of self. The shower and the coffee he drank forced him to recognise the here and now, and the idea that he had work to do that would help him get through another day: not that he had any idea of what to do.

His cleaning woman was due that afternoon, so Carvalho made a rapid check to make sure nothing was visible that Máxima should not see. It was while he was doing this he realised he had not even looked at his mail. He peered at the envelopes and divided the letters into those that were worth reading and those that were not. Almost all of it was junk mail, except for two items: one was from the savings bank, the other from his uncle in Galicia. Carvalho began with the letter from the bank. It was a current account statement: a hundred and seventy-two thousand pesetas. He felt in his jacket pocket for the fifty thousand Don Ramón had given him, and briefly wondered whether it would be better to deposit it in his current account or in his savings book. He looked for the book in a small money box he kept in the bottom drawer of a writing desk. Savings: three hundred and fifty thousand pesetas. Together with what he had in his current account, that made a total of almost half a million pesetas. After ten years' work, that was neither good nor bad. It simply meant that after another ten he should have reached a million, and would not die of poverty in old age.

Carvalho decided to put the money into his savings account. Somehow money in a current account is always more ephemeral, more at the mercy of a handy chequebook. It would be safer in his savings account. He counted the fifty banknotes again, then spread them out on the table like a gangster showing off. He picked them up one by one, stacked them in a careful pile, and fanned the air with them. After that, he put the notes in an envelope and stashed it away with his savings book. Next came the letter from his village. His father's younger brother had written to him in his almost illegible handwriting, with strange gaps between syllables and sudden bursts of high-flown rhetoric which made the meaning even more obscure.

Following a lengthy introduction covering health matters and memories of his father, Carvalho's uncle painted a not unskilful picture of arable despair: the harvests had failed. Then it was the turn of the unfortunate livestock: one of his cows had died after eating some grass it shouldn't have, or perhaps, who could tell, owing to poison administered by one of his neighbours. As if all this weren't bad enough, his wife was ill and he had sent her to Guitiriz to take the waters. A fortune! If Carvalho's father had been alive, he would surely have responded to such a dramatic situation, and so he and his wife were wondering whether he could perhaps see his way to helping out a bit, only if he could, of course, and without wishing to cause him problems of any kind. By the way, he was sending a dozen chorizos, two cheeses and a bottle of brandy by a slow but sure delivery man.

Carvalho let out a string of curses in Galician against families and mothers who would have them. He thought about writing a tough reply in which he told his uncle straight out about how stupid his father had been to share the inheritance with them, to help them as much as he could throughout his life, and to die with scarcely anything to his name. And all because he had gone off first to Cuba and then to Madrid and Barcelona, which meant the rest of the family saw him as Mr Moneybags.

But he did not do it. Instead, he scrawled a few lines telling them he was sending a money order for five thousand pesetas. He reckoned his father would have done the same, and that in so doing he was in some way reincarnating the old man. Carvalho's eyes grew misty when he remembered seeing his dad laid out cold and shrunken on the slab in the mortuary at a Barcelona hospital after he had rushed back from San Francisco. This was the second five thousand pesetas his father had cost him, the second cow he helped his uncle pay for in posthumous honour.

Carvalho had a lot to do before he met Bromuro again, almost all of it connected to his Galician roots. He drove quickly down the highway from Vallvidrera, deposited the money at the branch on Carlos III, then sent the money order from the post office in Avenida Madrid. A half-hour later, he was at peace with himself and with his future.

He left his red Seat coupé in the car park in Villa de Madrid square. He liked to park his car near the top of the Rambla so that he could stroll down it to Charo's neighbourhood. Carvalho walked in a leisurely way under the plane trees, stopping now and then to allow himself to be distracted by the most unlikely attractions. Patches of white and yellow sunlight filtered through the leaves of the trees on to the rare morning passers-by. Carvalho walked under the arcades of Plaza Real and the eighteenth-century atmosphere gave him an immediate sense of peace and harmony. He headed for a wide porch and walked up some marble steps surrounded by unpolished wood. A little old man in a chequered apron appeared at a door also made of heavy wood varnished a chocolate colour. When he saw it was Carvalho he opened the door and ushered him along a corridor lined with wallpaper featuring scenes from Pompeii. They soon reached a dining room done out in a pseudo English style, full of small plaster statues, ships in bottles and a display of faded brown family photographs in front of which two flickering candles floated in bowls. The room smelt of wax and boiled cabbage, and reminded Carvalho of childhood summer holidays spent in Souto in Galicia, with cows' muzzles peering directly into the family dining room from their barn next door.

Don Evaristo Tourón motioned to him to sit down, and immediately launched into gossipy memories about their native region. Carvalho was afraid he was in for another exhausting and impossibly complicated story about the wolves on Monte Negro which caused havoc throughout San Juan de Muro and sometimes even got as far as Pacios in their pursuit of Manolo the tailor's sheep.

'I came to talk to you about tattoos, Don Evaristo.'

'Oh, I see. You want to get a tattoo. I don't do them any more. You have to have a steady hand. A steady hand and the desire to do it. Nobody ever became a good tattooist if they did not enjoy doing them.'

Don Evaristo stood up to get a photo album out of a drawer in the sideboard. It showed his greatest professional triumphs.

'Look. Here's one I did for a man from El Ferrol. A fisherman on the cod trawlers. Look at this.'

The tattoo was a leafy tree that completely covered the man's chest. Instead of fruit hanging from its branches there were women's bodies. In another photo, an apeman was showing his flexed biceps with a tattoo of the statue to Columbus in Barcelona, and the motto: *Mercedes, I'll find you wherever you hide.* A third was of a teenager proudly mooning at the camera. Don Evaristo had engraved on his buttocks: *Exit only; no way in.* Don Evaristo sighed as he regretted yet again not having photographed the tattooed penis of a famous pickpocket. On the foreskin he had tattooed a cat. When it was pulled back, a mouse appeared on the tip.

'I'm telling you, Pepiño, I sweated as much blood as I spilt over that one. And you should have heard him howl. But he had balls all right.'

Carvalho asked him whether anyone was still in business.

'I tried to create a school here. But I failed. Who was it that used to want a tattoo? Sailors and crooks. Sailors aren't what they used to be, and the crooks don't want tattoos any more because they can identify them. I had an apprentice by the name of del Clot who was good. But he was a queer, and in that line of business he was constantly being threatened. The only one left now is a guy from Murcia. He lives up near the park. But there aren't many more in Barcelona. Tangiers: there are still a few there. And in Morocco in general. And some of the northern ports. Not Hamburg. Hamburg's got a big reputation, but there's nothing there. Rotterdam before the war. It had good tattooists then, very good ones.'

Carvalho asked him whether he had heard of the tattoo on the dead man's back.

'That sounds interesting. Before the war you used to get really educated people wanting tattoos. Once a kid from a good family who was in the Spanish Legion came to see me. He asked me to tattoo a motto in French for him.'

The old man went over to the sideboard again and came back with a notepad. In it he had written the best mottos he had come across.

'What does it say there, Pepiño?'

'*Ah Dieu! Que la guerre est jolie/avec ses chants, ses longs loisirs.*'

'That's right. He told me it was by a very good poet.'

Carvalho asked for the address of the tattooist who lived near Ciudadela Park. The old man could not remember the address, but drew him a map.

'You can't miss it. Besides, he's unmistakable. He's got a gammy leg and weighs more than a hundred kilos.'

Carvalho escaped as quickly as he could from the old man's effusive farewells.

'Tell me when you're coming and we can have pork shoulder. One of my brothers-in-law sends me the meat from Pacios. I'll keep it and you cook it, Pepiño. If only I could cook as well as you!'

Carvalho hailed a cab on the corner of Plaza Real and the Rambla. Ten minutes later he got out at the entrance old man Tourón had drawn for him. On the fourth floor a busy, irritable woman showed him into a small waiting room. There was barely enough room for Carvalho to squeeze in between a black plastic armchair and a table piled high with copies of the weekly *Semana*. A short while later, the tattooist's immense belly tried to make its entrance into the room. His head was still in the doorway, but his abdomen was almost pressed up against Carvalho's nose.

'Don Evaristo Tourón sent me.'

'Well now, that's good.'

'I'd like to talk to you about the tattooing business.'

'That's even better.'

The tattooist withdrew his belly and invited Carvalho to follow him. He disappeared into a small office that reminded the detective of the one in the hairdresser's where he had spoken to Don Ramón. The tattooist sat behind a desk and offered him a cheroot.

'They're mild. Perfect for this time of day. So you want to talk about tattooing. That's good. But the business itself is bad, real bad. Haven't done a thing since an Italian ship was in port about six months ago. Everything good is disappearing. There's no time for anything these days. In the past all a man needed to do was show a woman his tattoo and he was made. Now he has to show her something else straight away.'

He began to laugh, coughing and spluttering as he did so. Carvalho echoed him politely.

'I'm looking for a man who has a very curious tattoo. The motto reads: *Born to raise hell in hell.*'

The last ripples of the tattooist's laughter died away. He looked Carvalho up and down.

'You say you're a friend of Don Evaristo's?'

'We're from the same village in Galicia.'

'Well now, so you're from Galicia too,' said the Murcian tattooist without much enthusiasm. He studied Carvalho and waggled his head as though he were facing a real dilemma.

'That stupid tattoo,' he said at length. 'The cops have already been here asking me about it.' He did not take his eyes off Carvalho as he spoke. Carvalho did not flinch.

'The cops?'

'The guy with the tattoo is dead. And not a nice death.'

'Did you do the tattoo?'

'The cops told me not to talk about it without getting in touch with them.'

'Before or after?'

'They didn't say.'

'Well then, you can get in touch with them after you've told me.'

'Yes, I did the tattoo.'

He realised that by saying this he was opening some kind of door.

'Who was he?'

'I can see you know nothing about the business. Nobody gives their name here. Particularly if it's only a simple tattoo.'

'But you must talk about something while you work.'

'When I work I don't drink or talk.'

He burst out again with his spluttering cough, which he seemed to switch on and off without warning. All at once his face became as solemn as if he were at a funeral.

'Is this a loved one you're trying to find?'

'Let's just say I'm beginning to warm to him.'

'Oh! I can't say my heart's in it any more. It's a tough job. I scarcely make enough to get by, and I have to charge so much it scares off the few clients I might have.'

'Talking wears out the tongue. I'll pay you something to compensate.'

Carvalho took a thousand-peseta note out of his wallet. The tattooist held his hand out as far as his belly allowed, and waited for the note to fall into it.

'He was a tall, blond kid. He seemed like a foreigner, but he wasn't. He had some sort of accent, but it didn't sound like he was from Andalusia or Murcia. I've heard similar accents in people from Ciudad Real. Or he could have been from the south of La Mancha. Or from Extremadura. It was very odd.'

'Did he live in Barcelona?'

'No, he was just passing through. He told me he had worked in Holland. At the Philips factory in The Hague. That's all I know.'

'How long ago was this?'

'About eighteen months.'

'Do you remember anything else about his face or body? Anything that struck you at the time?'

'Nothing, I swear. And the information I've given you is more out of friendship for Don Evaristo than for the thousand pesetas. Friendship is a good thing. Why are you looking for that kid?'

'A premonition. I think he might be a friend.'

Carvalho sat on the terrace outside the Versalles. Bromuro was on the prowl for customers. He came to a halt in front of Pepe's muddy shoes and was told he could clean them. The waiter served Carvalho a gin and tonic and a plate of stuffed olives. Bromuro waited until he had gone, then said in a low voice:

'I don't have anything precise on that dead guy. But there's a helluva storm going on. The police raided everywhere yesterday and arrested lots of people. Whores and their pimps. Hundreds of them.'

'Maybe it's just a clean-up operation.'

'I've heard they're after anyone who has anything to do with the drugs trade. Lots of French pimps have moved in recently, and they're well organised. They bring their own girls, drugs, the lot.'

'What have the raids got to do with what I was asking you about?'

'There could be something.'

'Tell me.'

'I don't know anything for definite. But I've heard that the drowned man could have a connection with all this.'

'Does anyone know who he was?'

MANUEL VÁZQUEZ MONTALBÁN |||

'If I were you, I'd ask the girls. One or other of them must have gone to bed with him, and a tattoo like that isn't easy to forget.'

'How many girls do you reckon there are in Barcelona? Five thousand? Twenty thousand? A hundred thousand?'

'Charo could help you.'

Carvalho stuck another five-hundred-peseta note in Bromuro's waistcoat pocket.

'So how come they haven't picked you up yet?'

'And why not you? Or do you have special privileges?'

Carvalho replied with a smiling 'possibly', and stood up to go. He walked quickly to Charo's place. The caretaker was not there, so he had to run the risk of finding out for himself whether Charo was free or busy with a client. Although he had a key, he preferred to ring the bell. He thought he saw someone peering through the spyhole, and the door opened only a few inches. He heard Charo's voice:

'Come in.'

Carvalho walked down the corridor to the living room, with Charo following behind.

'I've got visitors, so take it easy.'

Carvalho could already see the visitors. Two women were moving around in the kitchen, preparing lunch or perhaps breakfast. Charo put her finger to her lips for him to be quiet, and pushed him towards the bedroom.

'They're two friends of mine. They just managed to escape being arrested yesterday and asked if they could stay a few days.'

'You're getting yourself into a mess. This place will soon be crawling with pimps, and the police will be next.'

'I couldn't just leave them out on the street.'

'Why not?'

'Go fuck yourself. Get out of here.'

'Listen. This is a serious business. These aren't normal raids. They're going after drugs in a big way, and all these girls are mixed up with people who deal as well. Besides, they're going to need to work: do you want them to bring all their men back here?'

'Why not? It's a big enough place.'

'And what will your select clientele say?'

'My clientele or you? What will you say?'

Charo was in passionate solidarity mode. It was like arguing with a statue to class consciousness. She was still wearing her negligee, and the dark lines stood out under her eyes. Her blonde hair with platinum highlights looked unkempt, desperately in need of a comb.

'Hello there, Pepe.'

Carvalho nodded as Charo's two companions came into the room. He thought he remembered that one of them was called the Andalusian: she was small and had flame-coloured hair. He did not know the other girl: she was good-looking and seemed very young.

'I was so scared, Pepe! First we heard the whistles, then they appeared out of nowhere like ghosts. Soon the place was crawling with them. They swarmed in everywhere.'

Carvalho went out on to the balcony of this new building, put up as a one-off in a district that had not grown in a century. Every so often the gap left by a property destroyed in the war provided the opportunity for a house like this to be built, its eight floors of boxes and glass towering above the red verdigris-stained roofs all around them. If Charo had listened to him and moved to a villa out in the suburbs, there would be none of this trouble. He went back into the room, where the three women were still talking nervously.

'As long as you're here, your pimps stay out in the street, got it? It's them the cops are after, not you, and I don't want Charo to get into trouble.'

'Don't worry, Pepe, they're already in clink.'

Saying this, the Andalusian girl burst into tears. Carvalho took Charo to one side.

'I need to know if any of your friends ever met a guy who had a tattoo on his back with the motto: *Born to raise hell in hell*. A young, tall man with blond hair. He had an Andalusian accent, though he wasn't from there, and he had been or was working in Holland.'

'The madams of the brothels are more likely to know something like that. If you're nice to these poor girls and don't upset them, I promise to find out.'

'Leave them here and come to my house until all this blows over.'

'Can I see my clients there?'

'Stop working for a while. You don't need the money.'

'How would you know? I'm not leaving this place.'

'I may have to go abroad. Just for a few days. You could move into my place while I'm away.'

'No chance.'

Carvalho shrugged and walked away, but Charo went after him.

'You've no reason to treat me like this. Who do you think

you are? This is my house and I do what I like with it. Do you pay for it? When have you ever given me a cent towards it?'

'Drop it.'

But Charo would not drop it. She followed him to the landing door.

'If I were in their position I'd want them to help me.'

'You're not in their position, but you're getting caught up in this.'

'I am like them. The only difference is I work for myself. Anyway, you're like them too, or almost.'

'Like who?'

'Like the cops.'

Charo showed she meant it by closing her mouth in a firm line. Carvalho did not know whether to slap her or turn his back on her. He stared intently while he made up his mind, and Charo could see the indecision in his eyes. She took a step backwards and looked him up and down challengingly.

'Find out about the tattoo.'

Carvalho was on his way downstairs when Charo leaned out of her doorway.

'Come tonight.'

'So we can sleep in the toilet?'

'Would you like me to come up to your place?'

'Drop it. I'll call by later.'

Carvalho set off in a hurry for Queta's hair salon. It was full of women and the buzz of conversation. Fat Nuria stopped combing through a client's greying hair to trip surprisingly lightly up the stairs to the office. Carvalho and Queta eyed each other. She was shaking a bottle of shampoo, but her huge eyes were fully fixed on the casual, determined way Carvalho crossed the room and headed for the stairs at the back. By the time he reached the office, Fat Nuria had warned her boss he was on his way. Señor Ramón received him with a hasty smile on his lips and a quizzical look in his eye. Fat Nuria stayed in the room, like a tiny but tenacious bodyguard, until Ramón signalled for her to leave. By then Carvalho was already ensconced in the small green armchair. When the girl's footsteps on the stairs had died away, he leaned forward and put a hand on the desk.

'This is getting too complicated. Yesterday's raids are linked to your dead man.'

'How do you know?'

'That's my business. Did you know this case had to do with drug trafficking?'

'I don't even have the faintest idea who the dead man was. Have you found out?'

'If I don't unearth anything definite in the next twenty-four hours, I'm going to have to go to Holland. There's a lead there.'

Señor Ramón's prefabricated smile slipped a little.

'I'll send you the bill.'

'Send me whatever you like, but don't come here again until you know something for sure. I don't want to get mixed up in this. Have they arrested your girlfriend? If not, they could at any moment. They've closed all the brothels. All except the really expensive ones. And the bars. Your friend is in danger.'

'She works in her own place, and for herself. Just like your wife.'

The two men stared at each other without blinking. Señor Ramón's freckles looked almost yellow.

'Listen. The cops are making a determined effort to clean things up. An ambitious prosecutor is involved, and it seems some important names have appeared linked to the drugs business. Very important. Do you get me? If those important people are rounded up, the smaller fry are done for. I'm paying you to run the risks, otherwise I would have gone and got the information myself. So get out of here, and don't make life difficult for me.'

'For now, I'll send you the bill if I have to go to Holland.'

The other man waved his arm in a way that was both an agreement and a dismissal. Carvalho went back down to the salon and stood in front of Fat Nuria.

'You move quickly for a fatty…'

Tears of rage began to form in her eyes. Queta watched them from her chair. Carvalho decided to leave his confrontation with her for another time. As he passed by, he sized up her charms once more. All the way out into the street, he was imagining a complicated erotic scene in which Fat Nuria was with Señor Ramón while he took Queta up into a hayloft like the ones in his childhood house in Souto. He laughed at the way that hayloft kept coming back into his erotic fantasies. All of a sudden a very different image filled the strange cinema screen he carried inside his head. Señor Ramón was staring in terror while he, Pepe Carvalho, was hitting him as often as there were freckles on his bloated, mangled face.

'Where's Ginés?'

'Which Ginés? There's four of them.'

'The cockiest.'

'Then there's only one. Go up to the fourth floor. And be careful, there's scaffolding everywhere.'

The building was nothing more than a concrete shell with metal girders. From a distance it looked as though it was peppered with the orange balls of the labourers' protective hats. Carvalho peered up at the geometrical structure at the bottom of one section, then began his climb.

'Hey, you!'

The foreman ran towards him carrying a hard hat.

'Make sure you wear this. There are lots of apprentices and they can knock your block off if you're not careful.'

Carvalho put the hat on. It was like being given the seal of approval for his adventure. The staircase was little more than a cement ramp filled with bricks to walk on. When Carvalho reached the fourth floor he paused to get his breath back. All around him, the horizon seemed to be bristling with half-finished constructions like this one, a forest of bulky skeletons growing inexorably. Below, a yellow curtain of smog lay over the city's industrial belt.

'Ginés!'

An orange helmet bobbed up. Underneath it was Ginés's white, rat-like face.

'Where's your detective's hat?'

'Have you got a moment?'

Ginés wiped the sweat from his thin eyebrows with his sleeve.

'Oh, Pepe, I'm so hot it's killing me! If only I could make a living with no sweat like you. What can I do for you?'

'I'm looking for someone. A drowned man. His body was found on the beach a few days ago and I need to know who he was. The cops haven't given any description. He had a tattoo: *Born to raise hell in hell*.'

'That drowned guy has caused mayhem. The cops have turned the neighbourhood upside down. It was only by a miracle my brother managed to stay out of jail.'

'Do you know anything?'

'Nobody knows anything. It's all connected to drugs and those French pimps who've brought whores in, from places as far away as the Cameroon. But there's no telling what it's all about.'

'Have you any idea what his name was?'

'No, and I've no way of finding out. I'm going to keep my head down for a couple of weeks. I'm going to take the children to the park and help my wife make balls of wool so she can knit me a winter pullover. Remember, I've spent seven of the last ten years inside.'

Carvalho had met Ginés when they were both in Aridel jail. Ginés was inside for breaking a security guard's arm with a chair.

'Do you think Felix might know something?'

'He was the first to make sure his hundred a.
were well hidden.'

'What about Valencia?'

'He's off his head. All the flowerpots at his place are i.
of marihuana. It's his wife who goes out to earn the dough;
he's on another planet. You'll have to try elsewhere, Pepe.
I'm keeping away from all my contacts: this looks bad, real
bad. When they close down all the brothels like they have
done, really close them down, that means it's serious and
won't go away overnight.'

'Let's go for a drink. Can you get out of here?'

'Yes, if I give an excuse.'

'What will your excuse be?'

'That I want to have a drink with you.'

Ginés strolled down the four flights whistling cheerfully.
He arrived at ground level while Carvalho was still
struggling two floors above.

'What about politics? When's that Khrushchev of yours
coming on his Vespa?'

'Khrushchev isn't coming on a Vespa or anything else.
He's dead. And I'm not involved in politics any more.'

'And there I was thinking I had a friend who would be a
minister one day.'

They reached the foreman.

'Listen, this gentleman is thirsty and I'm going to have a
drink with him.'

'What will I tell the contractor if he comes?'

'That's your problem.'

The foreman muttered something behind their backs.
Ginés stifled a laugh with his hand.

'That's right, arsehole, you go on moaning, that's why you're an arsehole. He's got an ulcer, you know.'

'So do you.'

'But I keep mine quiet by drinking.'

'Do they let you do what you want here?'

'They respect me. I'm the best. And they know it pays to keep me happy.'

Carvalho knew the stages of Ginés's drinking. At the fourth glass, he started talking about his mother. By the sixth, he was on to his legendary brother, his bosom pal. By the tenth, he was talking about what Carvalho wanted to hear. The bar was full of cheap plastic tables and calendars of chubby girls in bikinis. The floor was covered with a sticky layer of grime that not even Carvalho's impatient heels could dislodge.

'Ginés, if you were offered a thousand pesetas, couldn't you find out tonight who that drowned man was?'

'I'd do it for you, Pepiño. But I swear this is a bad moment. And my mother isn't well. I don't want her to suffer by getting banged up again. Try Bromuro. What he doesn't know about this...'

'Are you sure?'

'Positive. And if he hasn't told you anything, it's because there's nothing to know. Perhaps the cops are in the dark too.'

'But the drowned man had fingers, and there's something called an ID card.'

'That's true. But if they haven't said a name it's because they're being extra careful... You're not drinking, Pepiño.

You're making me talk, but you're not drinking. Typical Galician, that's what you are.'

Ginés's head was lolling back, and he was staring at Carvalho as though he wanted a fight. Carvalho ignored this, and thought everything over.

'You seem very worried. Was the dead man close to you?'

'No, but I'm interested in the case.'

'Shit, you look just like a film star when you say things like that. Real style. But you're a sly one. You haven't finished your second glass, and I'm on my fifteenth.'

'Do you have to go back to work?'

'I'll say I'm sick and I won't return. The house will get finished just the same. Come on, let's go and eat tapas in Calle Escudillers.'

'I can't. Really I can't.'

'Be off with you, then. I'll stay a while longer. I'm sorry, but I'm not going to scare my mother to death again.'

He was almost in tears.

'The last time it was my brother. They caught him in bed with his boss's wife and tried to beat the shit out of him. The boss and his sons. They attacked him with a hammer, but he fought back. You know what we're like, we may be small but we've got balls. Six months. They gave him six months for vagrancy. And he was lucky. But you should have seen what it did to our mother.'

'How's your wife?'

'She's been made pregnant.'

'Who did it?'

'It could well have been me. All I know is that's she pregnant. This big.'

Ginés held his hands out in front of him and burst out laughing. Carvalho recalled the dim outline of a tiny girl from Andalusia, bird-boned but with huge eyes, on the far side of the double wire mesh in the prison visitors' room. Ginés had leaned towards him and said:

'This is my wife. She's a real beauty, though she doesn't look it now. As soon as I get out I'll spoil her a bit, she'll come up a treat, and I'll be in clover.'

All that was ten years ago, and only Ginés had remained the same.

Carvalho dined on tapas in Plaza Real, then headed for Charo's apartment with two litres of beer in his stomach and heartburn from fried whitebait cooked in too much flour and oil. This time he did use his key, and as he opened the door he was confronted with the scene he had feared. One of Charo's companions was sitting on the sofa crying her eyes out, while a sharp, sallow-skinned young man paced up and down beside her. Charo was trying to comfort the crying girl; her Andalusian friend was in the kitchen.

'What are you doing here?'

'He's her boyfriend,' Charo tried to explain.

Carvalho pointed to the front door. The young man's sour expression gave way to the self-satisfied grin of a jumped-up mafioso. Carvalho glanced at the flashy rings festooning his hands.

'Put your cheap jewellery away and get out of here.'

'Why don't I stuff it in your mouth?'

Carvalho appeared to take no notice of this, but suddenly whirled around and chopped the other man hard across the neck. He staggered backwards, and Carvalho was on him, connecting with a right and a left to his face. Neither the girl's screams nor Charo's protests could stop him. Carvalho bent over the pimp, grabbed him by the hair, and beat his head against the wall. The pimp slid down until he was slumped on the floor. Carvalho went through his pockets, his waistline, under his arms, and the lining of his shoes. He took a folded switchblade from somewhere. Then he stepped back and from the middle of the room glared at the three women to prevent them protesting. Charo was paralysed by indignation and fear. The girl from Andalusia seemed to be preparing some sort of explanation; the other girl had her arms round her bloody and battered boyfriend.

'I told you your pimps were not to set foot in here!'

'I thought he'd been arrested!' moaned the tearful girl as she knelt beside her man. Charo kept saying over and over like a stuck record that Carvalho should go with her into the bedroom, because she had something to tell him. He pushed her away.

'The cops aren't joking. People are being swatted like flies, and here you are playing at sisters of charity.'

Carvalho led Charo out into the kitchen. He did not offer her the chance to complain, but gave her a stark picture of what was happening in the city. Charo began to be less frightened of him and more worried about what might happen to her if she got mixed up in what was going on. 'But in any case, that's no reason to treat that boy the way you did, Pepe,' she said.

'I can't stand pimps.'

'He's not a bad sort. He really loves her. She would have ended up badly but for him.'

'They need to understand things one way or another. Did you find out anything for me?'

Charo had been able to talk to only five madams. One of them from Calle Fernando thought she remembered a guy who had a strange tattoo, though she wasn't sure it was exactly that one.

'There's no brothel in Calle Fernando.'

'Well, in that short dead-end street nearby. I can never remember its name.'

'Is that where she lives?'

'No, she lives with her son in an apartment in La Ronda. Near San Antonio market. She told me that some time ago a man fitting the description you gave me went to the brothel a few times. He always asked for the same girl. One they call Creamy or Frenchy. She pretends she's French, and she's always carrying round creams to sell to her clients to make a bit extra. Apparently this girl told her he was a really strange guy with a very strange tattoo. But he's not well known round here. Nobody else remembers him.'

'How can I meet this Frenchy?'

Charo left the room, but came back a minute later.

'They say you should ask in a bar almost on the corner of Calle Fernando. It's one of the few they haven't closed, though the girls have gone.'

'OK, but I've got to go abroad for a few days anyway.'

Charo stood in his way in the kitchen door and kissed him on the mouth, then whispered in his ear for him not to be too hard on the others. Carvalho moved her aside gently and went into the living room. The young pimp still looked completely out of it, though the two women were busy trying to bring him round with wet flannels.

'When he's feeling better, turf him out. And if you two won't see reason, you're out as well. I've already told you, I don't want Charo mixed up in all this.'

Carvalho sounded almost amiable, so the girl from Andalusia decided it was time to deliver her sermon.

'Look, Pepe. There are lots of ways to say things, and you could have come in politely and said this is what I want, rather than getting violent about it. We're all in this together, and we have to help each other out, Pepe. Show a bit of solidarity…'

'As much as you like, but as soon as you've patched up our friend here, throw him out.'

'I'll come looking for you!' growled the pimp, angrily but in a weak, shaky voice.

'You'll need to get your eyes back first,' said Carvalho drily as he left. Charo was waiting for him in the doorway. They said nothing as they went down in the lift, or when they were out in the street. Carvalho seemed lost in thought. When they reached the centre of the Rambla, Charo hung on his arm.

'Where are you going?'

'Would you like me to come to your house? Are you going to be abroad long?'

Carvalho shrugged. They walked on until they came to the bar she had mentioned.

'I ask the questions. You keep quiet,' he warned her.

The raids had at least added some brightness to almost all the bars in Raval. As if by magic, the red and green lights had disappeared, and new hundred-watt bulbs made everywhere as garish as shopfronts. In the harsh white light, everything looked unfamiliar. Carvalho and Charo sat on a couple of high swivel stools up at the bar. Despite Pepe's encouragement, the barman kept his mouth tight shut. He knew nothing about the raids. Or what was behind them. But Pepe only had to glance despairingly at Charo, and she closed her eyes, leaned across the bar towards the barman, and whispered to him:

'Look, I'm worried about a girlfriend of mine. I don't know if they've picked her up or not. I'm talking about Frenchy.'

In Charo's body and voice, the barman heard the call of his tribe. Until then he had thought she was just Carvalho's sidekick. He knew his stuff, and almost without turning his head, made sure that nobody else was going to hear what he was about to say.

'Frenchy doesn't work round here any more. She went up to the Sarriá highway about six months ago. The cops have been up there too, but not as much.'

Carvalho left him a tip. The barman winked his thanks. When they were out in the street, a proud Charo hung on the detective's arm again and gave her verdict on all that had happened to them that evening:

'See? All you need is to be a bit friendly, and you get what you want.'

Carvalho nearly burst out laughing. Charo saw this, and sneaked into what she thought was a crack in the Pepe monolith.

'That's right, laugh! Laugh if you want to, I'm not going to charge you!'

Carvalho paid her no attention. He was considering the situation. One trail led to Holland, a specific job, a specific place. Another led to a woman on the game who had probably put away all her creams and pillows until the storm had passed.

'Charo, I'm off to Holland. Look for this Frenchy for me while I'm gone, will you? Be calm and patient about it, and make sure you take no risks.'

By now Charo was giving him short pecks on his shoulder-pad. Carvalho could feel her kisses penetrating this layer of protection and exploding all over his skin.

The plane landed at Nice for a stopover. Carvalho feasted his eyes on the spectacle of the mountains above the Côte d'Azur. Kilometre after kilometre of hills with villas nestling among well-tended vegetation. Carvalho compared this rational speculation of tiny paradises with the unbridled destruction of the Spanish coastline. His mind began to fill with the old logic that sought links between cause and effect, between good and evil. But as soon as this logic became demanding and insistent, an alarm bell went off in his head, and he dismissed all the arguments. He wanted nothing more to do with any analysis of the world he lived in. He had long since decided he was on the journey between childhood and old age of a personal, non-transferable destiny, of a life that nobody else could live for him, no more, no less, no better, no worse. Everybody else could go get stuffed. He had deliberately restricted his capacity for abstract emotion to what he could get from the landscape around him. All his other emotions were immediate, skin deep.

Ten new passengers boarded the plane at Nice, and the blue-uniformed stewardesses of the Dutch airline distributed them in the remaining seats. A leathery old woman sat next to Carvalho. She was wearing a typical flowery hat and looked neat and well turned out. She was in talkative mood, and Carvalho soon found himself immersed in an absurd discussion about why the salinity of the Mediterranean was dropping alarmingly. When the stewardesses started bustling up and down the cabin, he realised they must be in the last stages of the journey. He stood up and headed for the lavatory. He checked his papers. He had his Spanish private detective permit and the out-of-date ID the San Francisco police had given him eight years earlier. He made sure his Star revolver was fitting snugly in his shoulder holster. He took two switchblades out of his jacket pocket. One belonged to the pimp he had beaten up in Charo's apartment. He threw it into the lavatory bowl. The other was his, a magnificent Mexican blade he had carried with him ever since his adventures in Baja California.

He pulled up his trouser leg and slipped the knife into a sheath hidden in his boot lining. Then he returned to his seat. The old French lady had dozed off. Carvalho took advantage of this verbal truce to consider what had brought him on this journey. He could not get out of his mind the image of the faceless corpse of the man who was 'bold and blond as beer'. Sometimes he found himself filling the blank with other people's faces: Jean-Pierre Aumont in *Scheherazade,* or Tab Hunter. Or a blond Yves Montand with less clown-like features. All of a sudden, the words of the song Bromuro had mentioned came back to him, although they were still rather jumbled:

He arrived on a boat
With a foreign name
I met him in port at nightfall
His sad voice was filled
With a song that was yearning for rest.

That was it, more or less. He remembered how the song began:

Bold and blond as beer was he
A heart tattooed on his chest

The song was sung by a woman who had fallen in love with this handsome foreigner. With this handsome sailor who had spent one night, just one night, with her. Did that woman exist in the case of the tattooed man? He certainly had enough mystery about him for a woman to be caught like a bird in the branches of a tree.

Men of mystery tend to attract women, Carvalho told himself, almost out loud. Could the woman be Frenchy? It was significant that the man went with the same prostitute several times. Carvalho was sure that somewhere there was a woman, the singer of the song, who could tell him all or nearly all the secrets of the man who was 'bold and blond as beer'. The motto on the tattoo was surprising as well. One thing was a veteran of the Spanish Legion, full of scorn and literature, setting off between the wars on another adventure with his gun and some verses by Apollinaire. That would never happen nowadays, thought Carvalho, now that people have discovered they can only do what's possible. Nobody invents their life as if it were a novel.

> *That's why I search from port to port*
> *ask all the sailors for anything new*
> *Alive or dead, to him I'll always be true.*

The stewardess tapped Carvalho on the shoulder and brought him out of his daydream. She pointed to his seat belt. Her smiling, healthy face with a touch of rouge framed by auburn, almost red hair gave her a look hardly ever seen in Spain. Carvalho watched as she continued on her rounds, telling passengers about their belts, asking them to stop smoking or to raise their seat-backs. She was superb. Carvalho began to feel the kind of erotic urge foreigners feel when they identify a new city with new women. Every journey should lead to a surprising woman, a grand finale, the best terminus. Why not the stewardess? Carvalho tried to catch her eye, but she was surveying the passengers with a neutral, professional glance, and skipped over Carvalho like an object she had already checked and stored away.

Carvalho stifled his erotic impulse and instead stretched his head so that he could look out of the window beyond the old French woman and see the orderly green fields of Holland getting larger and larger as the plane began its descent. Awake again, his neighbour tried to engage him in talk about Holland. Carvalho told her he knew Amsterdam, Rotterdam and Leiden. The old French woman was going to her daughter's in Rotterdam. She was married to the foils teacher for the Dutch Olympic team. Was Carvalho going to Rotterdam?

'No, Amsterdam.'

Despite the fact that his real destination was The Hague, Carvalho had chosen Amsterdam as his base. Firstly because distances do not exist in Holland, above all the distances between Amsterdam, The Hague and Rotterdam. Secondly because Amsterdam was one of the cities in the world he adored, and something told him that the man as bold and blond as beer did not exactly fit into the mould of a Spanish worker stuck in the Philips factory at The Hague. His passage must have left traces in the splendid city of Amsterdam, and in particular in the red light district.

The plane landed at Schiphol airport, only a stone's throw from Amsterdam and Rotterdam. Carvalho knew his way around the airport, and headed straight for the bus station. His bus soon filled up with workers coming back tanned, moustachioed and loud-voiced from holidays spent back in their home countries. Turks, Greeks, Italians, Spaniards, Portuguese: a whole alphabet of poor European countries where life was hard. It was growing dark, but Carvalho still had time to take in the green, watery geometry of the Dutch landscape between Schiphol and Amsterdam. Fugitives from a dry country, the Turks had lost their initial boisterousness and gradually accepted the convention of silence imposed by this part of Europe, where everything looked as though it were drawn with a ruler.

For Carvalho, the old Schiller hotel was one of the attractions of Amsterdam. From the window of one of its slightly shabby rooms he looked out over Rembrandtplein. In the centre stood a statue of the heavyweight painter, displaying a serenity he would never have shown in his lifetime. If the Dutch could, thought Carvalho, they would turn Rembrandt's tortured paintings into eighteenth-century French pastels. Above the rooftops he could see the gilded figure of an angel with a trumpet on top of a clock tower in a nearby square. He decided to postpone his visit to The Hague until the next day. It was growing dark with Nordic rapidity, and he wanted to make use of the last daylight to re-acquaint himself with paths he had traced on previous visits along the canals down to the red light district, the Central Station and the port. Also, he did not want to miss having dinner in an Indonesian restaurant. He knew Amsterdam boasted two outstanding choices: the Indonesia or the Bali. The first of these was only two or three blocks from his hotel, and its Rysttafel was unbeatable.

Nothing in the world could stop him enjoying two glasses of genever, washed down with an equal number of mugs of beer, in the first tavern he found. Places like this in England and Holland appealed to their customers with the warmth of their wooden panels and well-worn tables, the space they offered for people to sit and talk, the time allowed for beer to settle into the contours of stomachs. Carvalho realised yet again that it is the small details that create the overall meaning of something. One of the things he had been most looking forward to on his journey to Holland was to be able to drink those two glasses of Dutch gin, washed down with mugs of beer. Genever, made from grain and juniper berries, is unclassifiable,

much less refined and elaborated than English dry gin.
You have to ask especially for it from the waiters, because
they consider it too rough for palates unaccustomed to it,
and prefer to offer English gin instead. There was a time
and a place for everything. Carvalho remembered the
ghastly amontillado he had been forced to drink so often
in California because there was no real Spanish sherry to
be had, the Californian burgundy or those Californian
white wines which were as similar to white wines from
Galicia as celery is to asparagus.

If there is room in the human body for two genevers
and two mugs of beer, there is room for four. In a spirit of
great self-sacrifice, Carvalho put this theory to the test, then
went out for a walk, happy to concede that the world, or at
least the Dutch corner of it, was as it should be. The waters
and the trees of the canals were dark, but the blood flowing
through his own veins was lit up by the alcohol he had
consumed. He walked along several streets, catching the
first glimpses of darkness in the bowl of night. Slow cyclists
drifted lazily past him, while cars sped along, trusting to the
survival instincts of anyone on foot.

The evening was cool, so Carvalho decided to return to
his hotel for his coat. The receptionist gave him his key, and
told him to wait a moment. From the far end of the foyer
an immense trench-coat appeared, topped by a tiny green
Tyrolean hat sporting a grey feather. A pure Ayran quickly
showed Carvalho his police badge. He spoke in English,
and asked whether he minded answering a few questions.
Carvalho went to sit with him in the same corner he had
emerged from. As if by magic, the man's hand suddenly

sprouted a small wooden box with two rows of tiny cigars the size of toothpicks. Carvalho took one.

'We remember you well.'

'It's been a long time.'

'Not long enough. You were here for two years as a security expert.'

'That was a political appointment.'

'Yes, I know. My colleague Rinus Kayser told me. He sends his regards. He could not come in person. How many days will you be in Holland?'

'Not many. Three or four.'

'The reason for your trip?'

'A sentimental one.'

'A girl?'

'Amsterdam. It's a city I love.'

'Hmm. Are you sure there is no professional reason for your visit? We could help you.'

'I don't work much these days, and when I do it's as a private investigator, as you would call it. I live in Spain now, and all the work there concerns investigating unfaithful wives.'

'You don't investigate unfaithful husbands?'

'In Spain it's the men who have the money to investigate their wives' infidelity.'

'Is it one of those cases that's brought you to Holland?'

'We also have motels in Spain. Adulterous couples don't have to travel as far as Holland.'

'OK. Anyway, you know where we are. We would be very upset if we thought you didn't trust us.'

Carvalho said goodbye to the cop with all the warmth

of his Celtic ancestors. He even accompanied him through
the revolving doors and out into the street. Afterwards he
went up to his room to go over the interview in his mind.
He had not expected things to move this quickly. Of course
he knew where to find them. In Holland you never see a cop
in the street, but there are as many police stations as there
are chestnut sellers in winter. He wondered whether they
would keep watch on him during his stay. He didn't think it
was very likely, unless the Spanish police had sent a report
before he had got here, linking what he was doing to their
anti-drugs operation. That did not seem likely either: most
probably it had just been a warning. We know you're here,
and by the way you no longer have any of the privileges of
a security expert sent by the US government. OK, message
received. Carvalho thought that was probably the end of it.

His determination to eat in an Indonesian restaurant
put an end to his deliberations. With every step he took
towards the Indonesia he could feel his appetite increasing.
The short ride up in the lift to the restaurant did nothing
to diminish it. Faced with the huge choice on the menu,
he decided there was only one option: the most expensive
Rysttafel. Anywhere else in the world, it would have been
heresy not to accompany it with wine. But in Holland it
was heresy not to have a couple of glasses of chilled beer.
When the small candles were lit under the hot plates for the
Rysttafel, Carvalho suddenly felt depressed. It was nothing
more than the typical sense of deflation that anyone dining
on their own tends to feel. Faced with the implications
of that, there was nothing for it but to eat a lot and well.
Within five minutes, the stomach starts its psychological

warfare with the brain. And as always happens on these occasions, it is the practical intelligence which wins out over the theoretical. The tongue serves as intermediary between spirit and flesh, and brings the two together with all the art of a pander with first-class honours. The sauces were based mostly on peanut, as ingredient or on the side. The wide range of stews and fried dishes combined perfectly with the bland taste of the long-grain Indian rice. And whenever Carvalho's palate began to suffer from an overload of spices or sticky sauces, half a glass of beer washed it clean and fresh, ready to undertake further magical research.

Many of the houses in Amsterdam's Jewish quarter are nothing more than their façade, retained in order to preserve the city's visual harmony. Behind that, most of them are empty, or have collapsed, and the façades are shored up to await the final curtain. This one was different. It was a noble building, with silversmiths' signs, the smell of money and efficient offices. Carvalho walked up two floors. He reached a door lit by strip lighting. In the centre of it was a brass plate: Mr Cooplan, Import & Export. Without taking his eyes off the door, Carvalho stretched out his left arm until it was touching a big Delft flowerpot. He lifted it a few inches with his fingertips, until he had room to feel what he was looking for. A key.

He thrust it in the lock without hesitation. He found himself in a brightly-lit corridor the colour of eau de Nil. The figure of a man dressed like a mannequin on the Champs-Elysées appeared from behind a frosted-glass door at the far end. As he came towards Carvalho, his features also took on the painted, stiff appearance of a mannequin. Although obviously taken by surprise, he walked confidently up to the detective, and stopped only a couple of metres from him.

Even his few grey hairs seemed deliberately put there to show off a bronzed, youthful face.

'What are you doing here?'

The man's gaze dropped to Carvalho's hand holding the key.

'You still have a key?'

'No, this is the one that was under the pot outside.'

The mannequin raised an eyebrow – just one, but with the practised ease of an actor at a crucial moment. He turned on his heel, then set off back down the corridor.

'Follow me.'

Carvalho ignored him. He started to open the doors into the offices lining the corridor. They were all neat and tidy, ready for the next working day. He stepped inside one that was full of filing cabinets. All the drawers were locked.

'You're wasting your time.'

The mannequin was in the doorway. The expression on his face must have been irony.

'Time is what I have most of.'

'What are you looking for?'

'Information.'

'There's no reason I should give you any. You don't work with us any more.'

As ever, Max Blodell spoke to Carvalho in a mixture of Harvard English and Colombian Spanish, reflecting the two countries where he had found it necessary to learn the language.

'Let me put it this way. Get out of here right now, Pepe. You're not welcome here. They don't like people who storm out the way you did. Now what are you doing?'

Blodell closed in on Carvalho. Pepe had a gun in his hand, and was aiming it at the lock on a filing cabinet. Blodell thought about wrestling the gun from the Spaniard, but decided instead to go for his own in his shoulder-holster. Carvalho did not give him time to reach it: he stuck the barrel of his automatic in the other man's stomach.

'Overreacting as usual, Max. Is Cor here?'

'No, he's working in Indonesia.'

'How could you bear to be separated from your great love?'

'That's all over and done with.'

'Didn't you succeed in setting up a homosexual branch of the CIA?'

Max took two steps back. He looked upset.

'I'll forgive you that, Pepe, if you leave right now.'

'I won't be long. But I need some information.'

'I can't give you any.'

'One good turn deserves another.'

'What good turn?'

'The one I always did you and Cor by not telling headquarters that you loved each other until death did you part.'

'Private lives…'

'You know that's nonsense. You know that as soon as headquarters find they have a homosexual on their books they treat him differently, and sometimes even use him for that.'

'You always were a creep.'

'I need just a few things, and no one will ever know I got the information here. It's not a very important case. Are you still in charge of Latino immigrants?'

'Yes.'

'Good. I'm on the trail of a Spaniard who worked at the Philips factory in The Hague. All I know about him is that he had a tattoo with the motto: *Born to raise hell in hell*.'

'Sounds like a verse from Milton.'

'It isn't.'

Max signalled for him to follow, and they went into the next-door office. Max looked in a file devoted to strange identifying marks.

'Your tattoo isn't here.'

Pepe mechanically checked some of the faces in the file, until he realised he was returning to his old habits, when he was in charge of this CIA office in Amsterdam together with Max and Cor.

'I'm sorry. I can't help you.'

'But you can. You might not know, but someone else could. Some former colleagues who might have seen the tattoo.'

'My informers won't be of any help. If they had seen something like that, they would have told me.'

'Yes, but it's not only your informers who have that kind of information. Tell me the name of a leader, one of those Spanish workers who has authority and knows everything, someone who's respected and asked for advice.'

'A communist?'

'Not necessarily. Almost better if he wasn't. They tend to be suspicious, and I don't have much time. A "born" leader who's not that involved in politics.'

'At the Philips factory in The Hague?'

'Right.'

Max led him into another office. He took a folder out of a filing cabinet identical to all the others.

'This man might help you.'

Carvalho noted down the name, age and place of birth of a gaunt forty-year-old with thin lips, square jaw and a high forehead exaggerated by a receding hairline. Max drew him a map of the factory and the workers' exits.

'This is where he comes out. He's nearly always accompanied by another man. I think they come from the same part of Spain. You're sure to see him there at two minutes past twelve. That's when they have lunch.'

'Have you had him followed?'

'Occasionally.'

'Is he a Red?'

'No, but he collaborates with them when he thinks it's a purely work-related matter. And the Reds seek him out too because he's got so much prestige.'

'Is he distrustful?'

'Very.'

'Anyone apart from him?'

'Not that I can think of.'

'How about asking prostitutes?'

'That's pretty impossible. There are so many of them and not all are registered with the police. There are private security people now who protect them and hide them. It was easy when they were just German or Italian, but now it's gone completely haywire – there's Turkish women, Greeks… even Spaniards.'

Max giggled at the thought. Carvalho put his notes in his pocket and headed for the door.

'Leave the key where you found it. No, better still, give it to me.'

'I'll leave it where I found it.'

'I hope this is the last time we meet.'

'That's not the sort of thing you should ever say.'

'Well, I'm saying it.'

Carvalho walked down the corridor trying to take in all the offices and to remember exactly what he had been doing there four years earlier.

'Cor was a good man.'

Something akin to emotion shone in Max's eyes.

'He's doing very well in Jakarta.'

'I remember he was there before, when all the Reds were being killed in '65 and '66. Why is he there now?'

'Reds spread like weeds. And even renegades still bear some traces.'

Carvalho reached out and brushed Max's cheek. Max recoiled as though he had been clawed at.

'I was never a renegade, Max. I was a cynical apostate. No more, no less.'

The northern sun proved Pio Baroja right. It softened colours rather than intoxicating them as the harsh brightness of the south did. This Nordic light brings out all the nuances in the sea of green, lends a sheen of age to the drunken roofs, and paints each leaf on the trees of Amsterdam with a different brushstroke. Carvalho had to make a great effort to leave the city for The Hague. For breakfast, he ate rollmops at a blue-and-white van outside the Central Station. As he munched his third slice of black bread with raw herring and onion, he could see the glass-sided boats manoeuvring into position as they set off to take tourists round the canals. He must not leave Amsterdam without taking the trip again himself, lying back and watching the city pass by above his head, a silent spectator at the ghostly parade of a sixteenth- and seventeenth-century city.

Dutch trains always seem like suburban ones. They are more like an open-air metro than a proper railway. People get on and off as if they were on an underground train, and the towns go by in the same harmonious, uninterrupted style against the backdrop of an unvarying landscape. Carvalho remembered the story he had heard from Carrasquer, a

professor of Spanish literature at Leyden University: Holland
has only one mountain, and that's only five hundred metres
high, so to avoid wearing it out the Dutch do not climb it,
but instead gaze at it like a national monument.

Carvalho's carriage was filled with quiet, self-absorbed
passengers. Every so often he caught the sound of a few
words of Spanish, Italian or Greek, and some in another
language he supposed was Turkish. But the placid Dutch
seriousness seemed to impinge on the southern Europeans.
In an environment where silence is so important, even
Southerners are silent. Or perhaps, thought Carvalho, they
are simply afraid of upsetting the Northerners' psychological
balance with the lewd phonetics of poor nations. In order to
blend in better, and to enjoy some Dutch tobacco, Carvalho
had brought a pipe. He soon noticed that the simple fact of
smoking it made him more detached, and helped him look
at other people and things with greater distance. He puffed
on his obedient appendage and the rising smoke sealed his
sense of well-being.

When he arrived at The Hague he decided to walk for a
while, from the station down to the main shopping centre.
He recognised a restaurant he had enjoyed the last time he
had been here: The House of Lords. He studied the menu
outside and resolved to come back and eat here if he had
the opportunity. Among the daily specials were snails
from Alsace and roast gigot of lamb, which made him feel
nostalgic. He had not eaten a proper gigot since he had been
in Dijon for the wine festival. He knew he could trust The
House of Lords to do it justice. He remembered a turkey
with pomegranate stuffing he had eaten among wood-

panelled walls that imitated an English club. The chef had been from Galicia too, he seemed to recall.

The lunch hour was approaching, so he hurried on to the Philips factory. While he was waiting for the workers to emerge, he flicked through his copy of the porno magazine *Suck*. The front cover seemed to be a homage to the carrot and its uses. As soon as the first men came out of the factory gates, Carvalho folded the magazine and put it in his pocket. He fell in with the labouring masses rushing in search of food, and soon heard Spanish being spoken. He discreetly followed two short, stocky men in their forties as they headed off determinedly towards the centre of town. He kept close behind, and as soon as they became separated from the others, caught up with them.

'Excuse me. I heard you speaking Spanish. I'm passing through here and wanted to eat somewhere where they serve food from back home.'

The two men looked at each other and shook their heads doubtfully, as if Carvalho had met them in Madrid and asked whether it was far to Barcelona.

'There's not much choice here. It's different in Rotterdam or Amsterdam. But not here.'

'Perhaps in that social centre.'

'Yes, perhaps you'll find some in a centre where he and I eat sometimes. We've just got to go and do something, but if you come with us we can tell you where it is, and we might even have lunch there ourselves.'

Carvalho could sense the plate of six delicious Alsatian snails slipping away from him, but thanked them for the offer as though he had suddenly been granted a pardon. He tried to strike up a conversation based on food. The two men replied with all the parsimony of Iberian Comanches. From their accents, Carvalho deduced that one was from Galicia, and the other from not far away.

'That's right. My friend is from Orense, and yours truly from León,' the less old and more talkative one told him.

They were walking in a hurry, with a precise destination in mind. They had already travelled several blocks, but still seemed to have a long way to go. All at once they came to a short, tree-lined street. Carvalho followed them across it. They came to a halt in front of a nightclub window. The female attractions were displayed behind the glass. Five or six young women from exotic locations (from France to Kashmir) were showing off their breasts to passers-by. In a corner, a girl was showing only one breast. Her artistic name was Finita del Oro.

'She's one of us,' said the man from León, choking with emotion.

'From León?'

'No, from Spain.'

'She's the best of them all,' the Galician crowed. The two men looked at each other, gazed one last time at their half-naked compatriot, and walked off back the way they had come. They had crossed most of the city just to ogle the charms of someone from home.

'Have you got your families with you?'

No, they did not. The man from Galicia was not married; the other one was, but his wife was back in León. He went home every two years and managed to make up for it.

'I behave myself here. For one, because I want my wife to

behave herself in León, so I do the same. And also because it's expensive to have fun and we're here to save.'

The man from León had already bought a flat in his home town, and was giving his daughter a good education: she was studying French and typing.

'Languages are very important. You realise that when you travel abroad.'

Now that his sexual itch had been satisfied, the man from Léon was talking freely. He had left Spain when he was already forty because the sugar industry in Léon where he had worked was in crisis. He thought you could live well in Spain, except in four or five provinces. 'People have it easy where you're from,' they both said when Carvalho told them he lived in Barcelona.

'But I come from Lugo.'

'Which part of the province?' asked the shy Galician, at last finding something he felt he could comment on.

'From Souto, near San Juan de Muro.'

'That's poor land. It's all very poor round there.'

Carvalho could scarcely remember how poor the land or the people were, but nodded energetically. He asked how they were getting along in Holland. Whether they didn't have any problems. The two men glanced at each other.

'We're not interested in politics. We're here to save a bit of money and return to Spain.'

'But are you treated all right? Does the Spanish embassy look after you?'

The two men exchanged looks once more, and when the one from León faced Carvalho again, he had the expression of a man being questioned in a police station. Carvalho guessed they thought he must be a Spanish cop trying to work out their political affiliation.

'I'm only asking because I used to have a friend in The Hague who worked in the same factory as you, but he said it was awful. We called him the Tattoo Man: he had a huge one on his back with the motto *Born to raise hell in hell.*'

The two men were listening closely as they walked on.

'Was he here a long time ago?'

'Two or three years.'

'What was his name?'

'I don't really remember. We used to call him the Tattoo Man, so we never bothered about what his real name might be.'

'What was he like?'

'Tall, blond, good looking. He looked like a foreigner.'

The Galician dug his elbow into his mate's side.

'That's the American.'

'Could be. A tall blond kid used to work here. We called him the American.'

'And he had a tattoo.'

'How would you know?'

'Now this gentleman has mentioned it, I remember it well. We once played a football match against the Spaniards from the Philips factory at Eindhoven. The American played for us, and I saw his tattoo in the changing rooms. I remember the bit about hell. I can't remember the rest, but I do recall that word.'

They reached the social centre, which was back close to the factory. It was not managed by Spaniards, and there was no sight of any Spanish food. Carvalho was served a strange sort of aubergine stew, which he recognised as a pale imitation of the Turkish *eman bayildi*. The waiter was Turkish, but he spoke a few Spanish words with an Italian accent, enough for him to communicate with both the Spanish and Italian workers. The man from León insisted on paying for a round of beers, brushing aside the timid, hesitant offer the Galician made. Then the three of them ate what was put before them.

'I can't remember the name of my friend the Tattoo Man. Or the American, as you used to call him. Could it have been Luis?'

'No, sir.'

The Galician knew what he was talking about, and began to speak with the authority of an expert.

'His name was Julio Chesma. He was from Puertollano, in Ciudad Real province.'

The man from León was not so sure about his family name.

'Julio, yes. But I wouldn't swear it was Chesma.'

'Chesma. Ches-ma. Believe me. When I damaged my hand here I spent three months in the office, and saw the records of half the company. Julio Chesma. From Puertollano. He was twenty-seven.'

'Listen to him, will you? He sits there quietly as though he isn't taking in a thing, then all of a sudden he's a real encyclopedia.'

'Did he quit here a long time ago?'

'He didn't stay long. He was one of those who soon get tired of factory work and look for something easier. Some people don't know they're born.'

'He went off to Amsterdam.'

Carvalho began to look at his fellow Galician like Robinson Crusoe gazing at the washed-up boat promising him his life back. The man had the mental recall of a great masturbator. He was aware he had won the battle over the man from León and that he knew things of interest to this half-Catalan gentleman. The price of his knowledge was to have it praised. Carvalho paid the price.

'You're the twenty-four-volume Espasa. What a memory you have!'

'He lived in Amsterdam at number sixteen, Rokin Street.'

He was overwhelmed by his success. He could not help laughing proudly at his own prowess, at the way he had impressed not only the workers' leader from León but this city slicker.

'How on earth do you know all this?'

The man from León was annoyed as much as astonished. The Galician explained that they had become friends through football, and that they had met up some Sunday afternoons in Amsterdam. He sensed that the other man was upset at not being the centre of attention any more, and threw him a lifeline: he questioned Julio Chesma's character, making him a scapegoat on the altar of morality.

'He was a lazy bastard.'

'You're right there,' agreed the other, catching the line.

'A scatterbrain,' the Galician went on, sacrificing an absent friend in order to keep in with the one sitting next to him.

'In Amsterdam he shacked up with a woman and found money from somewhere, though I've no idea where. He lived in a very nice boarding house in that street I mentioned. He had a room to himself with a bathroom and all mod cons.'

'What did he do?'

'He lived off women.'

The man from León saw an opportunity to refocus attention on himself.

'Lots of them do that. The women here think we're dying for it, so when they get together with a Spaniard or a Turk it's a serious business. It's easy to get into it, but you need to use your brain. Which is what your friend never did.'

'He wasn't really a friend. I knew him from football and he was good fun. You can't deny that.'

'His sort are always good fun. They don't make any demands on themselves, so they demand nothing of anyone else either.'

Carvalho couldn't help feeling a certain admiration for the man from León. He obviously had the ideology he needed to prevent him thinking his own life was a heap of shit. And by now he had the bit between his teeth.

'That's why they never feel under any obligation to anyone. So they don't make any demands, and they always seem wonderful. You, for example, are not married, but you help keep your mother, and you send money back so they can improve the house. If they need a cow, or a sister gets married, or someone falls ill, you chip in, however hard it might be for you.'

At this, the Galician's eyes turned misty. He nodded in agreement. Carvalho caught himself agreeing as well, remembering how he had contributed to his own family home in Galicia thanks to the two five-thousand-peseta money orders he had sent his aunt and uncle. But soon he was cursing himself and the other two as he reflected how pathetic it was for the three of them to be sitting in Holland, so pleased with themselves for having helped buy a cow or pay for a daughter's typing lessons.

'It's not easy being Spanish,' said Carvalho, to see what would happen. And something did happen. The man from León stared at him, and thrust his face forward. He put a hand on Carvalho's arm as though to get his point across more effectively or to convince him of his error. He said emphatically:

'But it's the best thing in the world. Right now if there was a war between Holland and Spain, I'd go back and fight to defend my country.'

He turned to the Galician, who still seemed to be lost in his evocation of cows bought and sisters married.

'I don't know about you, but that's what I'd do.'

'So would I, of course,' the Galician assured him. At the same time, he looked at Carvalho as if hoping that this knowledgeable gentleman would deny all possibility of war being declared between Spain and Holland in the thirty years, give or take a few, that the three of them had left to live.

'There's not much chance of a war,' said Carvalho, coming to his aid.

'Of course not, it was just an example.'

The man from León glanced at his watch, and told his companion it was time they were getting back to work. Carvalho accompanied them to the factory gate and shook hands with a warmth that took even him by surprise.

'Are you spending Christmas in León this year?'

The married man from León shook his head.

'No, it'll have to wait until next year.'

With that, he turned his back on Carvalho, followed by his friend. The only trips those two would be taking were to nightclub windows where their cheap thrills were purely visual and did not even offer any human contact. Some are born to make history, others to suffer it. Some are winners, others are losers. Carvalho felt a rush of blind anger towards his own countrymen. After a while, though, he began to feel angrier still at the phlegmatic Dutch cycling past: they had no need to go and work in the cane fields of Murcia or in the Cartagena refineries. He muttered, 'What an easy life you have!' so loudly it caught the attention of a gentleman with briefcase and tie, who gave him a look of smiling condescension. Carvalho felt depressed, but realised his body had not betrayed him, and was pointing him in the right direction. It was taking him unerringly towards The House of Lords, determined to allow his stomach to make up for the fake Turkish stew.

The burgundy cost an arm and a leg, but Carvalho would have torn off both if he had missed the opportunity to anoint the roast lamb with it. He had reached the restaurant just as the waiters were relaxing their professional demeanour and seeking refuge in that strange no man's land where waiters and cooks go between sessions. Carvalho's sudden appearance brought them flocking to his table. The only other customers were an Indonesian family. The woman had the dark beauty of a Gauguin portrait, and the two daughters held the promise of womanly charms to come. The paterfamilias looked like a badly worn Sukarno weighing five hundred kilos too much. As they were leaving, they all bowed to Carvalho, who tried not to make it too obvious he was avidly watching the splendid woman's exit from the restaurant. He watched as she swished her way between the tables, and then turned ninety degrees towards the doorway. This angle allowed Carvalho to ascertain that her profile was as pleasing as her back view. She opened her almond eyes in order to assess this minute examination by a foreigner. On similar occasions, Carvalho had often regretted not carrying with him a stock of those business cards where you can scrawl a passionate declaration of love and slip it into the apparently unconcerned hand of a woman restrained by the chains of erotic convention. He must try it some day. A shame he could not start today.

He tucked into the lamb without holding back. Well-cooked meat is first and foremost a tactile pleasure for the roof of the mouth. Roast gigot of lamb is the least elaborate way of preparing the meat. It does not have the fake comradeliness of gigot peasant-style, with potatoes and beans, or the all too often flat fanfare of a leg of lamb, or the purely visual pleasures of gigot with spinach. Lamb roasted this way is above all well-cooked and well-condimented meat. When the aroma of the burgundy hit the delicate skin of his palate and rose to fill his nostrils with the heady perfume of red wine, it was like having a velvet fluid wipe away the tiny wounds that the pieces of meat had caused.

Carvalho ate with the calm enthusiasm of all real, serious gourmets. His imagination was on fire, but his lips and face moved only to the slow chewing of the morsels he was consuming. Carvalho kept his emotions to himself partly because he had always felt that solitary pleasures could not be communicated. A pleasure shared can become a spectacle, but never one enjoyed in private. But there was another reason: showing too plainly how much enjoyment a meal is giving you has a direct influence on the size of the tip you leave. Waiters are subtle psychoanalysts. As soon as they see from your expression that you are approaching ecstasy, they ask you to confirm it out loud, and peer into the recesses of your mind and your wallet with the intensity of a soulmate who will not achieve their own orgasm unless you leave at least fifteen per cent tip.

Carvalho ended his lunch with a piece of ripe Brie, but then could not resist the temptation of crêpes with marmalade. He had two coffees and two genevers to wipe away the last traces of flavours that by now were more engraved in his memory than on his palate. He could not get this after-dinner moment of truth out of his mind.

'The best pleasures are always those of memory.'

He said this out loud, with the result that the waiter came over to see whether he required something more. Carvalho translated his witticism, but could tell from the waiter's condescending smile and the way he hastily beat a retreat that either he did not agree with Carvalho's philosophy, or he was fed up to the back teeth with this drawn-out meal, or had not really understood the ultimate meaning of the words. While the waiter offered this plethora of reasons for the lack of communication, Carvalho realised he must be rather drunk, because in normal circumstances he would never have dreamt of trying to intellectually seduce a waiter.

He left the restaurant without feeling he could ask whether his compatriot was still in the kitchen, even though on the previous occasion he had almost kissed him in gratitude for the turkey with pomegranate stuffing. As he strolled back in the general direction of the station, he glanced at the department store windows. It occurred to him to buy something Chinese for Charo. He walked down the arcaded streets of the centre of the commercial district and bought her a Chinese jacket imported from Hong Kong. After that, he headed straight for the regal quarter. A Dutch flag was flying from the town hall balcony, showing that a member of the royal family was in town. He gawped like a tourist at the imposing International Tribunal palace. Some animal with copious intestines had shat on the lawn in front of the iron gate. Carvalho's attention was drawn from the striking pile of dirt to the sight of a parrot on the shoulder of an old Dutch lady who had obviously been imaginative enough to exchange the habitual transistor radio for a real flesh-and-blood creature. Carvalho decided it was time to head for the station. As he walked, he realised that the day had been useful not only because he had learnt about the sexual problems of migrant workers, but also for something more than his excellent lunch. The body given up by the sea at Vilasar de Mar might not have a proper face as yet, but he did have a name and a few details on his curriculum vitae. In fact, Carvalho already knew the one thing Señor Ramón had asked him to find out: the man's name. All he had to add to the name for a face devoured by the fishes of the Mediterranean was the information he had gleaned from the Murcian tattooist and his workmate in The Hague. He could return to Spain with nothing more than this, but he felt he still owed something to this young man as bold and blond as beer. Something that drove him to continue his investigation in Holland as far as it would take him. A young man whose imagination could not accept the reality around him. The reality was that he was an immigrant worker. His imagination created another world beyond work, freed from the constraints of having to clock in and out at the factory every day. To escape the system he had no problem relying on women to earn money for him. Carvalho was scornful of pimps. He knew from experience they were the worst of the underworld. Just once he had met one with feelings, a prisoner who was expert at using toothpicks to bind up the legs of sparrow chicks which each May were found dashed against the paving stones in the yard at Aridel. Carvalho remembered the ponce's gentleness and patience as he whispered words of encouragement into the supposed ear of the tiny, terrified bird, while his clumsy fingers danced with all the skill of a surgeon round the bits of toothpick he used as splints, and the fine thread he bound them up with. That huge pimp was in jail for having beaten his whore to death.

But in the case of the young man bold and blond as beer there were some notable and pleasant differences. The most obvious was the hundred thousand pesetas Señor Ramón had paid him. Then there was that motto on the tattoo, the defiant cry of a Renaissance prince in the body of a migrant worker who had become first a pimp and then a faceless merman, an amphibious creature without features or identifying marks.

I ask the sailors where he might be
But none can say if he's alive or dead
And so the search means all to me.

Staring at her glass of liquor on the weary bar, the woman of the song continued her stubborn search for a man who had arrived on a ship with a foreign name, and had a heart tattooed on his chest. Carvalho was sure there was a woman like that in this case. Somewhere, though he still had no idea where, imprinted on a woman's skin were the most revealing features of the drowned man with no face.

Night was falling in Amsterdam. Carvalho cursed the fact that he had missed out on a day's sightseeing. He ate more slices of black bread with raw herring and onion. Cold beer would help the digestion. He had the bright idea of asking some young girls how to get to Rokin Street. It was relatively close by, near the station and his hotel on the other side of Dam Square. Carvalho decided to walk, although the tram that went to the museum quarter would have taken him right there. Rokin Street was beyond the Damark and Dam Square, and in fact came out very close to Rembrandt Square. In Dam Square there seemed to be some kind of shouting match between a group of hippies and a few angelic-faced youngsters wearing yellow plastic waistcoats and extolling family virtues. The hippies, like a tribe of Comanches fighting a losing battle against the palefaces, were clustered on the steps of Dam Square while the angelic host proclaimed the glories of patriarchy or matriarchy.

Carvalho reached number sixteen Rokin Street and went straight in. A flight of wooden stairs led up to a neon sign declaring: *Patrice Hotel*. A cleaner who had been almost invisible in the semi-darkness opened the door for him. He sat in the hall awaiting developments. The pieces of furniture looked typically Dutch, with that doll's-house style the good burghers of the city traditionally opted for. A woman who must have been Patrice herself came out, proffering a body that had the thickness of age but was given a lift by skilful corsetry. Her face had likewise been artfully restored to a semblance of beauty. Carvalho told her he had come from Spain and was looking for a relative of his. The family was worried because they hadn't heard of him in almost two years. Julio Chesma. The last news they had was that he had been staying in this boarding house.

'Here? I couldn't say. Wait a moment.'

She stumbled over her English. She left, then returned with a tall, well-built Dutchman who looked very much like the inspector who had questioned Carvalho in his hotel as only a tall, well-built Dutchman could.

'Mr Singel does not speak English, but he has a good memory,' Patrice explained as she told the man what Carvalho wanted. The Dutchman examined Carvalho with an affectionate disingenuousness. Not for nothing do Dutch children believe that Santa Claus comes from Spain. He replied in Dutch to Patrice.

'You see, my husband has a better memory than me. It's true, your relative was here. But he left two years ago and we don't know what became of him after that. He was an excellent person. Very neat and tidy. Yes, very neat and tidy.'

Carvalho could get nothing more out of the pair. Julio Chesma had been a good tenant. They knew nothing about his line of work, but he did seem to have lots of free time.

Of course he never received any visits from women. They had no idea who his friends were, men or women. It was the husband who supplied this information: Patrice merely translated it into English.

Carvalho expressed his satisfaction that they had such a high opinion of his relative.

'I suppose I shall have to go to the police. Perhaps they know something.'

The Dutchman almost answered him directly, but quickly checked himself and went on staring at Carvalho with his wide-eyed, childish Santa Claus look. His wife went through the motions of translating for him, and soon came back with his reply.

'Yes, perhaps the police would know something. They have a very good information network and keep a close eye on foreigners.'

Carvalho said goodbye. He walked back down to the street, then stopped outside a wine merchant's a few doors farther down. Looking round, he could see there was a bookshop across the street from the Patrice Hotel from where he could watch all the comings and goings in the hotel. He went inside, keeping one eye on a pile of books about 1920s design and the other on the door of the Patrice. He was taking a chance waiting for something to happen, because everything might be as normal as it had seemed, or perhaps the Singel family liked their sleep and would not leave the hotel until the next morning. Twenty minutes later and he had gone through just about everything ever written on design between the two world wars. He did not want to move to another row because from there he would not be able to see the hotel entrance. After half an hour, Singel appeared and aimed his identikit appearance towards Dam Square. Carvalho followed him. Singel was strolling along without a care in the world. In Dam Square he waited for a tram – long enough for Carvalho to hail a cab and ask the driver to wait a few moments. The driver was as hysterical as all cab drivers in Amsterdam are. He complained about having to wait and having to follow a tram. Carvalho gave him a ten-florin note and his resistance weakened. He got out of the car and busied himself under the bonnet just in case anyone objected to him being double parked. Singel's tram arrived and the taxi set off in pursuit.

They did not go far. The tram came out into Leidsplein. Singel got off and headed for a crowded pub next to a seafood restaurant, something unusual in a country where the gastronomic choice in fish is usually limited to rollmops or the smoked herrings found on stalls in every Dutch city and town. Looking in through the pub window, Carvalho could see Singel sit at a table where the sole occupant was a girl dressed like a hippy. Singel spoke urgently to the droopy girl, who had hair like a dyed-blonde Angela Davis, eyes that looked as though they had been made up with lumps of clay, and a body wrapped in a sheepskin that had probably been slaughtered and turned into clothing while she was already wearing it.

Their conversation did not last long. The girl got up and Singel followed her. From the doorway of a nearby cinema where they were showing *Fritz the Cat*, Carvalho saw Singel start to walk back the way he had come. The sheepskin with the girl inside crossed Leidsplein heading for Weteringschans. Carvalho knew all that Singel had to offer, but the girl opened up new possibilities, so Carvalho decided to follow her. Close to Leidsplein there was a small, lively district, like a smaller version of the red light area, full of restaurants, a few nightclubs and sex shops. The girl carried on through it and then turned right at a corner. In front of them appeared a strange church with a façade painted in psychedelic colours. The Paradise Club: a former church donated by the city council to the young people of Amsterdam. It had become a vast emporium that offered musical and artistic pop, a café selling hash cakes, a magazine and film library, and a shopping centre for the somewhat limited consumer capacities of the hippy world.

To get in Carvalho had to become a member. Two florins, plus entrance fee. This was a formality he had previously encountered only in live-sex clubs. All the different chapels of the church were crowded with the denizens of Hippyland, who spilled out on to the double staircase rising left and right to the meeting rooms on the first floor. The girl slipped in through the centre doors leading to the apse, where a rock group was playing, while behind them a screen showed shapes and colours intended to supplement their psychedelic chords. The apse itself contained an audience seated in sober rows, but in the side naves the floor was littered with a confused jumble of humanity which only occasionally responded to the music. The smell of marihuana filled the air. Carvalho could feel dozens of pairs of eyes on him. In his mid-season suit he looked like a neo-capitalist from Mars, and his hair ended neatly at his shirt collar. He was like a tourist lost in the Marrakesh souk. The girl was striding up to the front of the aisle, forcing her way through the crowd almost like a swimmer. She started to talk to a group of sad-looking youngsters. Carvalho leaned against a pillar to look less conspicuous, but kept one eye on the girl while with the other he casually surveyed the high altar. The group had been replaced by clowns who made no one laugh. Somebody passed him a joint. He took a ritual drag on it, then passed it on to his nearest neighbour. Through the smoke he saw the girl standing up, followed by two young men. One of them was wearing a sheepskin that must be the twin brother of the girl's; the other looked like a Wild West prospector without a gold or silver mine to lay claim to. Buffalo Bill and the two sheep sauntered back towards the main door. Just as they were about to step outside they whispered something among themselves and, with what for them was an extraordinary display of speed and agility, flattened themselves against the walls. A police patrol car had pulled up outside the Paradise, and the cops were busy hunting down suspects on the pavement.

Carvalho had almost nothing to be afraid of. He walked outside, and from the top of the staircase watched the cops doing their job. They had already arrested two Malayans, and one of them was chasing a black man up towards Leidsplein. So Aryans were off the menu, and although Carvalho was a dark-haired Celt he would probably not arouse the cops' hunting instinct unless he was very unlucky. The cop had been unable to catch up with the black man, and came panting back. They put the two Malayans into the patrol car and sped off along Sarphatastraat. The flock of sheep and their shepherd Buffalo Bill came to life again. They went past Carvalho and disappeared into the shadows to the left of the Paradise Club. Carvalho guessed they were heading for one of the cars parked there, so there was nothing for it but to repeat the 'follow that car' scenario. Luckily, the trio was drifting along on the wings of Nirvana, which gave him time to find a taxi and sit in it waiting for them, his wallet lighter by another ten florins.

They were driving a 2CV painted in bright colours and plastered with pacifist stickers. The car went down Vijzalstraat towards Dam Square. Then it went up Damark until it turned sharp right into the maze of narrow streets leading to the red light district. They parked perpendicular to a canal, and Carvalho paid off his taxi. He stood waiting until they moved off on foot into the heart of the red light area. Nearly all the windows on the main street were lit up, and women sat posing for clients in front of attractive-looking beds. Only the bright red and purple lights gave an exotic touch to their quiet, almost wifely wait. Peeping Toms and ordinary passers-by peered at them briefly and looked away, because it was plain that the women did not like being stared at like monkeys in a zoo. Some of them were standing in the doorways, showing off their peroxide hair, their high boots and miniskirts, their bored, scornful expressions.

The three youngsters went into a takeaway pizzeria. Carvalho leaned on the counter and ordered a steak tartare sandwich and a beer. The shepherd and his sheep grazed on pre-cooked pizza. Buffalo Bill glanced at a pocket watch he had taken from what looked like a Wells Fargo saddlebag. The watch must have told them there was no hurry, because they also leaned on the bar in their usual dreamy way and began to talk among themselves as if they had the whole night before them. Carvalho asked for a sandwich with various tiers of cold meat, lettuce and boiled egg. He had another beer and struck up a conversation with the waitress. She was not much to look at but was all there in the right places, with mounds of auburn hair that looked as solid as her thighs above a pair of uncomfortable-looking boots. When he discovered she spoke only Dutch or English, Carvalho pretended to be a visiting Frenchman. No, it wasn't a very busy night. At weekends the area filled up, but mostly with tourists. Either foreigners or Dutch people from the interior who were venturing into the hell that was Amsterdam. As she said it, she added a touch of irony to the word 'hell'. Carvalho asked her the obvious question: whether she got off work late, and whether she had anything to do afterwards.

'I've got lots to do.'

'Bad or good?'

'That depends,' she said, laughing.

Carvalho could get nothing more out of her. She had a lot to do, which was good or bad depending on how you looked at it. It was obviously a defence mechanism that the waitress employed at least twenty times a night, so Carvalho decided on something more neutral and ordered another mug of beer. The three youngsters were still taking their time. Now they were drinking cups of coffee as if it were water, although the coffee in the pizzeria was as strong as espresso. Then Buffalo Bill consulted his watch again and they moved off. Carvalho let them leave. He glanced at the young girl under the pizzeria lights and saw she was neither ugly nor beautiful, but quite the opposite. By which he meant that she had acquired that neutral look with which liberated women defend themselves from becoming looked at as objects. They had certainly succeeded in their aim of not looking erotic any more, but Carvalho prophesied that they would soon create a fresh convention among their male partners, and in the near future women objects would become anti-women objects or women anti-objects.

With the look of a thief in a butcher's shop Carvalho paid a fond farewell to the waitress's thighs. The three others were strolling towards the central canal in the heart of the red light district. A circle of onlookers had gathered round a Salvation Army band singing its hymns of praise or dire warning on the very threshold of the hell that was Amsterdam. The prostitutes watched the Salvation Army's virtuous display from their shop windows. The uniformed musicians had been joined by some local housewives, who were protesting meekly about something that had given their neighbourhood its character ever since the days of Adam and Eve, when it first grew up alongside the port of Amsterdam and the Central Station, which brought in their endless quota of people with hungry loins. Curious onlookers and the down and out contemplated this piece of musical theatre with the condescending air of a football crowd being entertained by a Samoan wedding dance performed by a group of sensitive teenagers just finishing high school. The trees, the lights reflected on the water of the canal, the serene architecture of the surrounding houses, the polite reserve of the watching prostitutes, and the silent passers-by all contrived to make the red light district the opposite of sordid. In this context, the Salvation Army's thunderous hymns sounded like pasa dobles at an end-of-year student party.

The three youngsters seemed to tire of the spectacle. Buffalo Bill was definitely the leader. He looked down again at his watch, and they set off along the right-hand side of the canal, peering into the entrances to live-sex clubs, porno cinemas or the so-called Museum of Sex, which in fact was one of the most successful stores in the whole area. They surprised Carvalho by going in. This did not seem to fit in with their hippy lifestyle or the habits of the locals. It was as if a bohemian Parisian were to visit the Lido or go on an excursion to Versailles or up the Eiffel Tower. Perhaps they were just being kitsch, and wanted to find sexual gadgets they could laugh at or admire for being so naive.

Carvalho walked round the small museum and went down into the basement. If he had been on his own he would have bought a leather sadist's outfit that would have brought laughter or tears to the eyes of Charo, who had seen it all before but still found it hard to control her bladder when it came to laughing or crying. Then Buffalo Bill glanced at his watch again, and shepherded the other two out of the shop before they had time to look at anything. A group of French tourists was filling nearly all the gangways laughing hysterically in a way Carvalho would have thought possible only from a gaggle of Madrid matrons born in the back of beyond and brought up as strict Catholics. Idiocy and repression know no frontiers.

The three of them left the brightly lit canalside street as though they wanted to get out of the district altogether. They suddenly disappeared down a short alleyway on the right. Carvalho plunged after them, hurrying in order to keep them in view. They had speeded up, as though they wanted to gain time or get somewhere else quickly. The alleyway was in darkness, but Carvalho could just make out the girl running rather than walking away from him. Then he saw the two men stop, turn and come towards him. Carvalho looked over his shoulder and saw two more hulking individuals closing in behind him. He was like the ham in a sandwich, caught between the two men on one side and Buffalo Bill and the hippies on the other. He chose what seemed the easier option and charged head down at Buffalo Bill. He thrust his hand into his pocket. Carvalho succeeded only in butting Bill's bag rather than his body. He did manage to bring his open knife out of his pocket, but that was not much use either. The hippy sheep kicked him on the top of his skull. As Carvalho fell to the ground, the other two men reached him. He defended himself as best he could on his back, protecting his groin with his hands and kicking out in all directions. Someone kicked him twice in the ribs and he was forced to curl up into a ball. The two giants grappled for his legs and immobilised him. A foot began kicking his face. Carvalho tried to stand up. To his surprise they let him. As he struggled to his feet he could feel blows raining all over his body. One punch to the side of his head lit the dark street with flashes of light. The punches and kicks seemed endless. He had lost his knife, so there was nothing for it but to surrender.

After one particularly vicious punch, he dropped to the ground again.

The beating stopped. The four men said something to each other. They searched his pockets, then examined his papers. Two of them lifted him under the armpits. A third grabbed him by the feet and between them they started to carry him out to the end of the alley. Carvalho guessed they could be taking him to one of two places: either to the canal or to a car parked alongside it. If they threw him into the canal, they could either bind him hand and foot or drop him just as he was. If they tied his hands and feet he would have to struggle so hard he forced them to dump him on dry land rather than leaving him to drown. He half opened one eye and saw they were carrying him towards the edge of the canal. They were discussing something. It sounded as though they were worried about being seen. Carvalho could feel their arms grip him more tightly. He was preparing for the worst, but the three men were simply swaying backwards to gather strength, and he suddenly felt himself flying through the air. He fell two or three metres, and all he could think of was to shut his mouth to avoid the slimy canal water choking him. He hit the surface with a sudden cold shock, and allowed himself to drop down through the water. Fighting off his fear and repulsion, he swam along underwater. He could not see a thing, so he shut his eyes as tightly as possible. The stinking water filled his nostrils. He held his breath as long as he could, and tried to aim for the canal side. One of his hands came into contact with the slimy wall. It felt like the scaly skin of some wet, horrible animal. He searched until he could find a crack to get a proper handhold, then stayed under water until there was no more air left in his lungs. As he rose slowly to the surface, it felt as though they were two stones weighing him down.

The damp air hurt as he gasped for breath. Keeping his head low in the water, he tried to spot his attackers on the canal side. There seemed to be no one around. In the darkness he could make out the even blacker shadow of the bridge the canal disappeared under. Slipping underwater once more, he swam towards it. When he surfaced again, he was underneath the arch. He clutched at a crack between the bricks and decided to wait until he had a reasonable possibility of emerging unscathed. Everything was quiet except for the sound of water dripping from his soaking sleeves. His adrenalin had warded off the cold until now, but he suddenly realised his teeth were chattering. He was revolted and scared, but above all felt sorry for himself. He imagined the underside of the bridge infested with man-eating rats, and was so terrified at the thought that he forgot about his safety. He sought desperately for places in the brick wall above him, and used his fingertips to haul himself up, although the water soaking his clothes made him twice as heavy as usual. He could smell the acrid stench of canal water on his skin, his hair and his clothes. His wounds were burning, and one of his eyes was almost completely closed.

His head reached the top of the wall. He heaved himself up and collapsed face down on the side of the canal. He was breathing more easily now, but felt colder by the second. There was complete silence, broken only by the sounds of distant traffic. He decided to try to stand up. He succeeded, and stood still, waiting for some sort of reaction from his attackers. Nothing. As he set off running, he was deafened by the noise of his soaking shoes squelching on the pavement. As more water poured off him, he was able to run more quickly. His clothes were stuck to his body like a corset. He was in no state to hail a cab or even to return to his hotel along the main streets if he did not want to end up in a police station.

He felt exhausted, so sat on a short flight of steps leading down to a shop in a basement. He saw old newspapers sticking out of the tops of the rubbish bins. He pulled some pages out, took off his jacket and shirt, and began to dry himself with them. Every so often he rubbed a bruise or cut and muttered a curse. He wrung out the shirt and bundled it up in one of the bins. He tried to squeeze as much water as possible out of the jacket, then put it back on, raising the lapels to cover his chest. Then he took off his trousers and underpants. When he saw his private parts hanging down, he could not help but laugh. This was not the moment to be arrested as a flasher. He threw the pair of underpants into the bin as well, then dried the rest of his body. He wrung out the trousers as best he could and put them back on. The jacket and trousers were thick enough not to appear soaked through. He dried his hair and feet, then ran his fingers through his hair to comb it.

If he stuck to dimly lit streets, nobody would be able to tell he had almost drowned. He had left his revolver in the hotel, so he was completely unarmed. He walked towards the start of the canal, opposite an imposing neoclassical building lit by the lamps of a leafy square. He did not want to reach the square itself, but hoped he could take the first street on the right that descended towards Waterloo Plein. He heard the sound of a car behind him, and dodged down another flight of steps until it had gone by.

A few seconds later, a police patrol car glided past. The cops got out, and Carvalho saw them disappear through a brightly lit doorway. He spotted a narrow, dark street that came out a few metres this side of the police station. Just what he needed. He walked towards it, watching intently to make sure there was no sign of movement in the police station doorway.

He slipped into the street and headed for Waterloo Plein, hoping that by keeping moving he would regain some warmth and take his mind off the stabbing pains that seemed to be coming from all over his body. The closer he got to his destination, the more confident he felt. He met a couple who opened and closed their mouths in mute astonishment. By now his eye had almost completely closed. He skirted Waterloo Plein and went on towards Rembrandt Square. As soon as he caught sight of the open space in the distance he let out a great sigh of relief.

He flung himself in through the hotel's revolving doors. The amazed receptionist handed him his key and stammered out a couple of concerned questions about what had happened to him.

'Some people tried to rob me, and in the struggle I fell into the water.'

'Have you informed the police?'

'Yes, of course. It was them who brought me here.'

The receptionist accompanied him to the lift, emphasising how lucky he had been.

'Amsterdam seems like a quiet city, but at night the canals get filled with bodies. You had a lucky escape.'

When he was in the lift, Carvalho slumped against the side, his mind a complete blank. The menu for the hotel dinners was pinned above the instruction panel. It looked promising.

Carvalho opened his eyes. He was almost sure that there was somebody else in the room. At the foot of his bed he could make out the same inspector who had interrogated him the previous day. Now he was staring at him concernedly. Carvalho could not return the favour because one of his eyes was throbbing violently.

'They gave you a good going-over.'

Carvalho shrugged his shoulders. A stabbing pain in his ribs warned him not to do that again.

'You know the city. It's surprising you let yourself be jumped on.'

'They tried to rob me.'

'So the receptionist told me.'

'Did he call you?'

'You passed out in the lift.'

Carvalho opened his pyjamas and saw bandages and plasters on his wounds. He could also feel something sticky on his bad eye. Someone had patched him up.

'Was anything stolen?'

'No.'

'Would you recognise your attackers?'

'No. It was completely dark, and it was all over very quickly.'

'It's odd. Odd that they should throw you in a canal without tying you up.'

'They thought I had passed out.'

'But anyone who has passed out can wake up in a cold bath.'

'Maybe they were kind hearted.'

The inspector came closer to Carvalho. He sat in a chair next to the writing desk.

'It would be much better if you were straight with us. You were in the Paradise Club last night.'

'How do you know?'

'You became a member. We know the names of all the Paradise Club members.'

Carvalho wondered how many cops there had been disguised as hippies among the dreamy crowd in that particular paradise.

'Did you make any friends in there?' asked the inspector.

'I went dressed as a Martian, but they were in ordinary clothes. No chance of any small talk.'

'Did you smoke?'

'At my age you can't get used to that kind of thing. I'm almost forty.'

'Me too.'

'So you know what I'm talking about.'

'No, I don't. But that doesn't matter. What did you do when you left the Paradise?'

'I went to the red light district.'

'Did you go in any of the shop windows?'

'No.'

'Did you get drunk?'

'No.'

'Where were you attacked?'

'As I was going past an alleyway. They either pulled or pushed me into it. Four of them. They beat me up, and I pretended I had lost consciousness. They threw me into the canal. I waited until they had gone. Then I climbed out. I dried myself as best I could with sheets of newspaper and walked back to the hotel.'

'Why walk? We always have patrol cars in the neighbourhood. Or at the very least you could have got a taxi.'

'I was stunned. From all the blows. I wanted to reach the hotel, so I came walking back like a robot.'

The inspector seemed to be more interested in looking round the room.

'This hotel needs redecorating.'

'But it's still very pleasant.'

'Mr Carvalho, did you come to Holland on business related in any way to drugs? I don't expect you to tell me the truth. I just want to warn you.'

The inspector's finger was pointing at him accusingly.

'The Dutch state has sufficient resources to create its own security mechanisms. We don't need any foreign interference. Still less from somebody who isn't even officially one of us any more. You're a loose cannon, Mr Carvalho.'

'I guess this isn't the first case of a tourist getting beaten up and given a bath in a canal.'

'No, but you're a very special tourist. For example,

normal tourists go and make a complaint to the police after an assault. I suppose you don't want to do that.'

'No. I'm only in Holland a few days, and I don't want to complicate things by getting involved in a police investigation. Besides, they didn't take anything. I was only carrying American credit cards, Carte Blanche and Diners, and about forty florins.'

'You've still got them. They're rather wet, but still usable. Which means they didn't even steal the forty florins that were in your pocket.'

'Perhaps it wasn't enough for them.'

'We've come across cases where people have been drowned for less than twenty.'

'Unbelievable.'

Carvalho did not want to seem too smart, or to behave like a Chandler character facing a stupid, brutal LAPD cop. Among other things, because the inspector was not a stupid, brutal LAPD cop and he wasn't a Chandler character. The inspector stood up.

'This is the second and last warning. If you get mixed up in anything else, we'll take drastic measures. By the way, Inspector Kayser sends his regards and hopes you get better quickly.'

'Tell him I'll pay him a visit before I leave.'

'When will that be?'

'Probably tomorrow. Or the day after.'

The inspector left the room. Carvalho rang down to reception to ask whether he had been seen by a doctor. He had, and apparently there was nothing seriously wrong with him. He was to stay in bed for a day, and if he had any problems, feeling dizzy for example, he was to call at once so he could be taken to hospital. Carvalho lay back on the plump pillows and drank half of the glass of water that was on the bedside table. Then he hauled himself out of bed to see whether he could stand up. He knelt down and slowly straightened. So far, so good. He could feel pain in several parts of his body, and his eye stung like hell, but apart from that, nothing seemed to be broken. He lay back on the bed, relieved. He called reception again and asked them to fetch his suit and take it to the dry cleaner's. The receptionist himself came to get it. He asked how Carvalho was feeling, and promised his suit would be as good as new in a few hours. Carvalho ordered a fresh orange juice. It appeared with American alacrity. He drank it down, then sank back on the pillows. He did not want to fall asleep, but could feel a wave of tiredness coming over him. He closed his eyes, and almost immediately thought he could feel the slimy grip of the canal waters on his body. Grey rats were swimming towards him, their whiskers bristling above the water as they closed in on him. Carvalho was threshing about trying to stop them biting him. But he couldn't make any noise, because his attackers were still up there at the canal side, listening for any sign that he was still alive.

He was awakened by a knock on the door. He slowly realised where he was. He had slept for almost two hours since he had drunk the orange juice. 'Come in!' he shouted. The doorknob turned, and in the doorway stood none other than his old friend Singel.

That was Carvalho's first surprise. The second was the fluent English that Singel greeted him with, apologising for disturbing him, and asking him how he was. As before, Singel kept looking at him with his wide-eyed, angelic smile, like someone who has discovered a mysterious being from outer space. The smile was either a nervous tic or the sign that he was a public relations expert.

'Mr Carvalho, I'm going to spare you the trouble of asking questions and sum up the situation as clearly as I can. You have obviously made the connection between the visit to us yesterday and the warning you had last night. That is all it was, a warning. You are well aware we could have left you at the bottom of the canal if we had wanted to.'

The seriousness of what he was saying in no way altered his guileless, beaming expression. He went on in the same tone of voice:

'A few hours ago, a policeman came to see you. I'd like to know what you talked about.'

Carvalho was unsure that this was a different person asking him questions. Singel behaved just as politely as the inspector. Possibly they wanted to know the same things.

'I told the policeman what I wanted him to hear. And I'll tell you what I want you to hear.'

'We've been thinking that your interests do not necessarily clash with ours. Perhaps we were a little hasty yesterday, and you are looking for your Spanish friend for reasons that don't concern us.'

'I'm quite sure they don't.'

'So what are they?'

'Let's just say I've been hired to find Julio Chesma. I'm a private investigator, and there are reasons to believe that Julio Chesma and the body of a drowned man washed ashore on a Spanish beach are one and the same. A client has asked me to confirm his identity. A tattoo the drowned man had on his back is what brought me to Amsterdam. When I got here I learned his name and where he was staying. Now I need to know what happened to him from the moment he arrived at your boarding house to the moment he died. I'm not interested in whatever business he got mixed up in. Just what his life was like in those months. Nothing else interests either me or my client.'

'What relation do you suspect there was between your friend and me, for example?'

'I can imagine lots of things: drugs, the white slave traffic, smuggling tulips or Delftware abroad. Or you two could be masons, or part of Opus Dei.'

'Opus Dei?'

'I know what I mean.'

'It's true your friend had some business dealings with us. And of course we would prefer you not to try to get to the bottom of them. Perhaps it would be wiser if we collaborated. We'll give you the chance to find out how he lived, but the information will have nothing to do with the deals he did with us.'

'What sort of information?'

'Women, for example. He liked them a lot, but at the same time almost always managed to keep business and bed strictly apart.'

'It sounds like we have a deal.'

'You have no choice. You could probably go to the police and tell them about this conversation. All you would gain by that would be to have me arrested, but that won't get the Dutch police very far. They already know where I live, and anyway I have a dozen alibis. For you it would be different. If you go to the police, you might save yourself from a drowning in Holland. But there is water everywhere. And people die on dry land too.'

'I understand.'

'Perfect. Then I'll start by telling you all I know. Your friend stayed at the Patrice Hotel until a year ago. From time to time he took trips, but strictly for business. A year ago he became a permanent resident in Holland, also for business reasons. We heard about his death three days ago, through a channel I'm not going to tell you about. We don't know the details of his death: from what you've said it seems it was an unfortunate accident. Is that enough?'

'No. You've reduced months of his life to a few sentences. I'd like to hear a fuller version.'

'I could give you some addresses here in Amsterdam.

But I don't want you to go poking around with the police on your tail. You can get all the information you need in Rotterdam. Can you stand up?'

'Yes.'

'Go out into the street?'

'Yes.'

'Then you really were lucky. OK. Tomorrow take a train to Rotterdam. At three in the afternoon climb the tower that looks out over the docks. It's a very pleasant tourist atraction. I don't know if you're aware of it, but Rotterdam is the biggest port in Europe. Most people think it's Hamburg, but that's not the case. Don't go right to the top. Stay on the middle level. Go to the west side and stand by the handrail enjoying the magnificent view of the comings and goings in the port. Leave the rest to me.'

'I hope you aren't thinking of throwing me off the tower.'

'We respect truces and agreements.'

All of a sudden Singel's voice lost its curt, didactic tone. Instead it was as though he were visiting someone in hospital.

'Take care and you'll soon return hale and hearty to Spain. What city do you live in?'

'Barcelona.'

'A lovely city. My wife and I used to spend our summers in San Feliú, a small town on the Costa Brava. Do you know the Edenmar Hotel?'

'There are thousands of hotels.'

'We used to really enjoy it. But now we've changed destination: we prefer Yugoslavia. Nature there is so wild and beautiful, although the country is less well adapted to tourism than Spain. By the way, isn't the Barcelona team manager a Dutchman?'

'I think he is.'

'That's right, Michels. He's a great guy. He may not be a brilliant strategist, but he gets results. He was the one who turned Ajax into the best club in Europe. He discovered Cruyff, Neeskens, Keizer. Did you ever see the great Ajax team play?'

'When I was here last they had trouble even tying up their boots.'

'Recently they have become the best team in the world. Their style of play is quick and direct. The star of the team was Cruyff, but I almost preferred Keizer. He's a tough, aggressive player, but clever with it. Like that English player Best, but stronger.'

Singel went on to pour scorn on Feyenoord, Ajax's eternal rival from Rotterdam.

'Feyenoord is like the city it comes from, it has no class. All the Second World War bombings destroyed its character, now it's a nondescript place. But Amsterdam is beautiful, it's all character.'

By now Carvalho had realised that the other man was not making fun of him. He had simply changed register, and was following the conventions of his new topic in exemplary fashion. It therefore came as no surprise when his visitor stood up and said:

'Don't hesitate to ask us for anything you need. My wife and I will be very happy to see to it. If all you went through yesterday has left you feeling rough, call us. We'll find a discreet doctor. No point in creating a scandal over this, is there?'

Singel raised a hand to the side of his head to say goodbye. He walked carefully out of the room, as though trying not to make any sound that might upset the convalescent patient in his hospital bed. Carvalho refused to lie there thinking about what he had just been part of. He was hungry and needed some visual stimulation too. He got out of bed and put on his clothes.

A young man born to raise hell in hell leaves a steady job with an international company to devote himself to shady business. That shady business was drug trafficking. There could be no other explanation for the link between what Singel had insinuated and the raids in Barcelona following the discovery of the drowned man's body. Singel claimed he had not learned of Chesma's death until shortly before Carvalho arrived in Amsterdam. On the other hand, a small businessman in his attic office in a nondescript hair salon in Barcelona hired Carvalho to find out who the drowned man was. The two things did not fit. The heart of the mystery now was the reason for Señor Ramón's involvement. He was willing to pay a hundred thousand pesetas simply to confirm the identity of a drowned man, something he could easily have done via the police. But Señor Ramón had no wish to get involved with the cops, and obviously did not know anyone who could do so without a risk.

Carvalho had made it a matter of personal pride to find out what had happened to Julio Chesma's body between Rokin Street and the beach at Vilasar. He wanted to know why Señor Ramón was so interested. Carvalho walked towards Leidsplein, uncertain whether to have dinner in Bali or to try to find a restaurant in the area he had seen the previous night when he was following the hippy sheep. When he reached the Leidsplein, he went into the pub where Singel had met the girl. Even at this time of day it was almost full, both the main downstairs room and a sort of mezzanine which had room for only one big round table. Four or five people were sitting round it, staring at the others below. Carvalho sat with his back to the wall at a table where he could see out into the square and also enjoy the sight of the drinkers around him. Next to him sat a hippy couple with their children. Beyond them was a quiet office worker who was engrossed in his newspaper as the bubbles of foam on his beer gradually settled. Carvalho knew that in the afternoon he could get only a snack here, and also knew how demanding his stomach could be. The atmosphere in the pub lent itself only to chatting with friends or sitting watching the world go by. He wanted more than that: he was on his own, and needed entertainment.

He walked across the street to the cinema and bought a ticket. They were showing the B-film: a Dutch short called *The Hair Salon*. Carvalho could not follow much of the dialogue. The plot seemed to concern a hairdresser assistant's virginity. She goes to her boss's weekend cottage with her work colleagues and their boyfriends. Things warm up, and they all end up in bed. The recalcitrant virgin fights off all attempts to storm her temple, but eventually decides to satisfy her lonely boss. Her lonely boss, impotent but very human, tells her in a fatherly way not to expect anything he cannot give. The girl seems to take this very calmly, but the next day, bloody Monday, she wakes up as wild as a female orang-utan on heat. She has a fight with her mother and is on the verge of a nervous breakdown. She leaves home. Out in the street, she calls her boss from a phone booth and in floods of tears tells him something. As far as Carvalho could work out, there was no happy ending. Verdict: a crass film typical of lamentable Dutch film-making.

In the break Carvalho went out into the foyer. There were a few hippy-looking couples who had brought their offspring to the early show partly because they did not know what else to do with them and partly because *Fritz the Cat* was a cartoon. But as soon as he saw the opening scenes, Carvalho thought perhaps they had brought them along to offer them some sex education. Fritz the cat was a crazy dropout dedicated to bringing sexual revolution to the dope smokers among the New York intelligentsia and social revolution to Harlem. It was too cynical even for Carvalho. He came out feeling depressed and at the same time desperate for a fuck. He went down the street where he had followed the hippy girl the night before. He chose a Greek restaurant. He ordered lamb grilled with sage and a bottle of Paros wine. He finished with an excellent Toulomisso cheese. He hardly noticed what he was eating, and became worried about his state of mind. Foreign cities always offer the promise of fresh pleasures. But as soon as you scratch the surface, you discover how impenetrable its people are, how trite the situations you find yourself in. If he wanted a fuck he would either have to pay for it or engage in a lengthy verbal skirmish that might end in nothing. Carvalho was fed up with all the conventional foreplay, all the persuasion that was needed. It should be automatic. A man looks at a woman, and she says yes or no. Or the other way round. The rest is culture.

Carvalho glanced at the faces in the restaurant to see whether any of them might respond to this kind of direct appeal. Not a single attractive female face. He lowered his normal standards and concentrated on a middle-aged woman eating at a table with a short-sighted adolescent. She would do in an emergency. Carvalho stared at her broad face, waiting for their eyes to meet. They did, and the woman started a ghastly flirtation, alternating banter with the teenager with sidelong glances at Carvalho. Pepe soon realised he was doing nothing more than pandering to her taste for mental escapism. Another notch on the gun of his platonic conquests. Nearly all women are the same everywhere.

He was annoyed that nothing more was going to come of it, so stopped playing the game. He left the restaurant, still savouring the taste and aroma of sage. After walking around aimlessly for half an hour he found himself on the steps of the Rijksmuseum. These days he was allergic to museums, perhaps to compensate for the way they had enchanted him in the past, the way he had once adored their cathedral-like silence and the ecstasy produced by all the painters held in such high esteem. He would give the whole of Rembrandt for a shapely woman's arse or a decent plate of spaghetti *alla carbonara*.

He walked to the Paradise Club. He had to renew his

membership, as the previous card had been ruined by the canal water. This time he did not head for the apse, but went up to the first floor. There in a big room a few youngsters were reading magazines or trying to make collages out of cut-up photos. A few more were standing at a counter with the same world-weary look of all those he had seen downstairs the night before. He walked across the library and reached the counter, where a hippy couple was selling cakes. Hash cakes. Carvalho saw it as a dreadful reflection on the state of the art of cooking. What hope was there for young people who did not know or want to know how to eat properly? In order not to die before he had yielded to this devilish temptation, Carvalho bought a vaguely Arab pastry. It tasted of aniseed, almond, flour and something strange that could just as easily have been mare's sweat or divine ambrosia. He cursed the miserable motherfuckers who could have perpetrated such a monstrosity, then went on with his exploration of the upper floor of the sanctuary. In another room they were showing a Gregory Peck film to another bunch of hippies, sitting on folding stools or slumped on the floor. The film was *To Kill a Mockingbird*. By Gregory Peck's fourth facial tic, Carvalho had seen enough. He went back down the staircase and into the main nave. It was exactly the same scene as on the previous night: the same music, the same psychedelic effects, the same shit leading to the same nothing. And all the while the cops kept watch on them inside and out, as though they were sheep being led to the fold. For a moment, Carvalho considered scanning the room with his one good eye to see if he could spot Buffalo Bill and his flock. He could not help thinking that someone was deliberately fooling all these poor people who thought they had heard the bells of freedom. Where exactly were they headed?

The next morning he got up late. He looked at his eye in the mirror. The swelling had almost completely gone. It was not so much a black eye as a cut that now appeared clearly in between his eyelid and eyebrow. He used a piece of cotton wool to try to wipe off as much iodine as possible. His eyebrow still felt uncomfortable, but it was not really a black eye.

The journey to Rotterdam seemed endless. Unusually for him, he had bought newspapers: the *New York Times* and *Le Monde*. He had not read a paper in two months, but it looked as though not much had changed. If he had not been on the receiving end of all the nonsense he read about, he would have dismissed it as a freak show of madmen and crooks: all the rich and powerful deserved to be locked up and the key thrown away. He did not even get to the *New York Times*: the first three pages of *Le Monde* were more than enough. He preferred to stare out at a landscape that repeated itself endlessly, or to study the faces of the other passengers, who also seemed endlessly the same. For hours now, he had not been able to get the image of Señor Ramón sitting on the other side of the desk out of his mind. His sallow, freckled skin, the sly look in those small hard eyes of his, like some predatory animal. He had found out all that Señor Ramón had asked of him, and yet there were lots of questions he still wanted answered to his own satisfaction. If the journey to Rotterdam seemed so interminable, it was because he had the feeling that most of the answers to these new questions were no longer to be found in Holland. Carvalho was obsessed by this investigation in the same way as in the past, whenever he was trying to find the answers to a puzzling case. It was as if he were regaining an old, disturbing ability: the capacity for enthusiasm.

Coosingel Street started from close by Rotterdam central station. It went straight down to the port. The entire centre of Rotterdam had been rebuilt after the war, drawn in straight Dutch lines that emphasised how new it all was. Carvalho took a taxi to the riverside. He wanted to take a trip on one of the small boats that ferried people round the vast docks, and while he was doing so mull over the crazy logic of the case. He climbed aboard a Spido launch and found he was sharing it with a group of noisy schoolchildren, eager to discover as many new worlds as there were piers and warehouses in the docks, where ships from all over the planet were anchored. The colour of rust alternated with whitewashed hulls and the jumble of thousands of cranes settling like birds for their noonday rest. An old, smoothly running port where what was most impressive was its size and how smoothly it ran. A port without the legends of a Hamburg or a New York.

There was as much about the relation between Singel and Señor Ramón that did not fit as there was about the relation between Ramón and Queta's hair salon. An old man did not have the aura of power he had without there being something bigger behind him than a ladies' hairdresser. The most logical conclusion was that he was part of the same network in which Singel and Chesma also figured. In Amsterdam Singel hid behind the Patrice Hotel sign, just as in Barcelona Señor Ramón concealed his activities behind Queta's Hairdressers. The two men obviously used a front in the same way. But how were they linked to Chesma? Why did Chesma have a face and name for people in Holland, while remaining a question mark for Señor Ramón?

The launch was passing in the shadow of a huge Japanese liner. The schoolboys made slanty eyes and called out to the seamen on board in a language specially made up for the occasion. Then there was a succession of dry docks where they could all reflect for a few moments on how dead ships were being transformed. They stared in silent respect at the rusting hulls and their hasty skeletons, as if attending an autopsy. Even the schoolkids fell silent at the sight of how the wrecks were being gutted. Beyond the ships, the July sun made white shirts blaze. Carvalho had seen how the Rotterdam locals liked to sunbathe, stretched out on the wide green banks of the canals or enjoying the lunchtime peace and quiet on public benches. Charo had probably gone for a swim at Castelldefels or the Swimming Club. A tan was useful in her line of business, and Carvalho himself loved the contrast between the brown parts of her body and the surprising white of the rest. Perhaps Señor Ramón had hired him when he already knew the answer. But why? Why take such an interest in a return journey whose start and finish he already knew?

By the time the tour was over, there was already a photo waiting for him of the moment he had stepped on board. Carvalho bought it, and then headed for the watchtower standing high above the warehouse roofs. He followed instructions, and stayed on the observation platform beneath the top floor. Rotterdam stretched out to left and right in a maze of docks and piers, a forest of cranes which from this vantage point looked like small threads on some vast tapestry conceived by a pointillist painter anxious to convey his sense of the still life composed by trade and industry. Green, blue, white and red ships. Black ships that seemed destined for evil. Ships heading north, but mostly ships heading south. Carvalho could feel the urge to set sail rushing through his veins.

He was early for his appointment. He was almost alone on the platform apart from a Japanese couple in one corner busy photographing each other with the port as backdrop. Then he saw a woman in her thirties walking along the platform. One gloved hand followed the rail round, while she continued to stare out to sea as though she wanted to have a constant panorama of all that was going on down below. A pair of binoculars hung from her well-endowed chest. She had a long nose, a broad, freckled face and a mass of shoulder-length red hair. She was wearing a green sleeveless dress, and her skin looked as though the tan was artificial, or perhaps it was just the characteristic bright pink that redheads suffer from. Her legs were inviting, although her ankles betrayed the passage of time or the fact that she had bad circulation. Carvalho felt a fleeting desire, but almost at once it seemed crass and destructive to start to want a woman he would never see again. The woman reached the point where Carvalho stood leaning against the rail. To carry on with her tour of the platform she would have to walk round him. She came to a halt only a few inches from Pepe's body. She turned and looked up at the face of the man standing in her way. Her lips moved and she said in hesitant Spanish:

'Are you the man sent by Singel?'

S he said her name was Salomons. The widow of Cees Salomons, she explained. They took the lift down to the ground. While the attendant was busy with his levers, she whispered in Carvalho's ear:

'Is it true Julio is dead?'

'So it seems.'

'That's dreadful.'

She seemed genuinely upset. She strode out of the lift in front of Pepe and led him towards a Volvo parked at the foot of the tower. On their way to one of the least new districts of Rotterdam neither of them said a word. She came to a halt in a tree-lined street. At the far end a canal was visible. She opened the front door to an apartment block, then they went across an internal garden where a few girls in bikinis, bearded young men and straw-blond kids playing with a rubber ball were all out enjoying the sun. The widow Salomons opened her apartment door, and Carvalho found he was directly in a light kitchen-dining-room. A staircase led off it up to another floor. She gestured for him to take a seat on one of the stools that went with a high white lacquer table. She sat opposite him. In the centre of the table between them lay a wicker fruit bowl full of glistening Mediterranean fruit. The widow Salomons seemed to be lost in thought: she stared blankly at a stainless-steel kettle on the unlit stove.

'It's dreadful.'

'Did you know him?'

'Yes, I knew him well.'

She raised her head to the ceiling. Tears were welling in her eyes. As she stretched, he could see she had a thick but beautiful white throat.

'Very well.'

The tears poured down. Carvalho started to play with a grapefruit that seemed to have been polished with a cloth. The oranges and lemons were just as shiny. The widow raised her head again, and Carvalho sank his visual fangs into her beautiful white throat. He had the fleeting impression that she must have taken a course run by the Actors' Studio in Rotterdam. She wept like Warren Beatty in *Splendour in the Grass*. It was all so staged that to Carvalho her grief seemed to be delicately poised between the theatrical and the cinematographic. It takes all sorts, he said to himself, and began to peel an orange. The widow Salomons got up to fetch him a plate to put the peel on. Carvalho remembered an old joke he had heard from a professor of French literature, Juan Petit: 'Imagine that one of Jean-Paul Sartre's angst-ridden characters is in mid-crisis when he hears his doorbell ring. He goes and answers: it's the man from the electricity company. If he has enough money to pay, he's fine. He can go back to his metaphysical angst. But if he can't, his metaphysical angst goes out the window and an everyday angst takes its place.' Professor Petit had been as lucid as he was scary, sitting there clutching the vaporiser he used all the time to control his asthma attacks.

'I'm sorry. I'm making a fool of myself.'

Carvalho made an ambiguous gesture which she interpreted as giving her permission to carry on sobbing her heart out. There they were again, huge, heavy teardrops racking her body. Carvalho finished the orange and got up to wash his hands under the kitchen tap. Through the window he could see the sun-worshippers curing all their bodily and spiritual ills thanks to the oldest and most reliable god of all. He leant his backside against the sink, gazing at the picture of desolation offered by the widow Salomons and the bits of orange peel on a small Delft plate.

'So you knew him well?'

'Yes, as I already told you. I can't help it, I'm upset.'

'I'm sorry, but there's nothing I can do about it. I'm interested in learning a few things about my friend. His relatives are worried. They haven't heard from him in almost two years. The last letters they got were from Amsterdam.'

'After that he lived here in Rotterdam nearly all the time.'

'Here?'

'Here.'

'Was he still with Singel?'

'Yes. No, I don't know.'

'You don't know what?'

'I don't know if his friendship with Singel did him any good. But it did give him the chance to make a break. Do you follow me? He was someone who was born to be something more than a factory worker at Philips.'

'Nobody is born to be a factory worker.'

'You know what I mean. He was naturally intelligent. He had a quick mind. Come and see.'

The widow Salomons got up and climbed the staircase. Carvalho followed. At the top was a landing lined with books, prints and real paintings. Off the landing was a bedroom that was also full of books. Under the window was a work desk. Out of the window Carvalho could see the sun-worshippers still performing their silent rites.

'He read almost all of these. And don't think that they're easy books. He could read English almost fluently: he had taken an intensive course in Amsterdam. How could I describe him? He was... deep.'

'Profound.'

'Yes, that's it. Profound. He reflected about things. He always thought everything over a lot. And he was a rebel.'

As she talked about Julio Chesma, the widow Salomons paced up and down the room, cupping her elbows in her hands. Within ten minutes Carvalho had an excellent picture of him. He was born in Puertollano (province of Ciudad Real). A polluted, horribly polluted town, insisted the widow. Dreadful pollution. Naturally, he was an orphan, perhaps in fact because of that pollution. Raised in an orphanage, naturally. Everywhere he had been he had left traces of his brutal, futile sense of rebellion. The Spanish Legion, naturally. Petty crime and prison, naturally. He had found a girlfriend in Bilbao and that was the first time his feet had been on the ground. He studied at evening classes, then decided to work outside Spain so he could see something of the world, to discover what lay beyond the horizon.

'He was never going to stay at Philips for long. He couldn't get used to this,' she said, making the gesture of clocking in with a card.

'Were you the first woman he got close to in Holland?'

'No, I suppose not. After the Philips factory he went to Amsterdam and found work as a doorman at a live-sex club.'

'A doorman?'

'Well, he used to be in some of the acts. And in that line of business, you know, you meet lots of people, not all of them honest.'

'In other words, he fell in with crooks.'

'No, not exactly. Singel told me you already knew all about it. I don't think people who sell drugs are necessarily crooks. That depends on the drugs. If it's heroin or cocaine or opium, that is criminal.'

The widow was speaking without looking at Carvalho. Just like everyone else, her ideology justified her own way of life.

'Did Chesma meet you through Singel?'

'No, the other way round. I got to know Singel and all the rest through Julio. Two years ago. He came to Rotterdam often on business. I don't know how, but he had got hold of a pass for meals in an artists' centre. It's cheaper, and the food is decent. I always eat there. I work organising the artistic festivals of Rotterdam, in the Doolen, just by Central Station. We met at the restaurant there. I was fascinated by the huge gap between what that boy was and what he could be.'

'So you entered their organisation.'

All at once she was on her guard.

'Singel told me I wasn't to answer anything about that kind of thing.'

'I simply wanted to know if Julio was a strong enough personality to drag you into something illegal.'

'I did a few things. Only a very few, and above all to keep him from doing them. If he had been caught, they would have thrown him out of the country or put him in jail. Can you imagine Julio in a jail?'

'I can imagine anyone in a jail.'

'Some people wouldn't be able to stand it.'

'You could count them on the fingers of one hand, and there are something like three billion people in the world today. All of us fall into two groups: those who go to jail and those who might go to jail. That's the secret of success of all politicians everywhere.'

'But some people are especially sensitive. Julio was one of them.'

'Beware of people who are especially sensitive. They're capable of cleaning out the worst latrines in the filthiest jails in the world.'

'You didn't really know him.'

'OK, go on. Julio shows up, you fall in love. You see him off and on. He gets you involved in the drug business. You get him involved in the literature business. Fair exchange: you get money and he gets culture.'

'I never made a penny out if it! I only did it to protect him!'

Carvalho felt a desire to arouse sincere anger in this woman who seemed so good at playing a role without realising she was doing it. The secret of seduction lay in the wide, soft bed with its red-and-white sheets. All the rest was literature or an ideological mask to disguise the most basic instinct of all.

The widow Salomons sat on the bed. Her legs were slightly splayed, revealing the firm consistency of her thighs. Carvalho feasted his eyes.

'Bit by bit he started staying longer in Rotterdam. He made two or three trips to Spain before going back the last time.'

'Have you any idea how it occurred to him to have that tattoo done?'

'No, but perhaps he thought it was his personal motto. Nothing he got involved with ever ended happily. He was thrown out of everywhere, but he was a leader. A born leader.'

'Why did he decide to go back to Spain to live?'

'I've no idea if he meant to stay there. Our relationship gradually fell apart.'

'From your side too?'

'No.'

It was a faint, uncertain 'no', as if on a low flame.

'No,' she said again, more firmly. 'I still loved him. A lot. But he wasn't someone to settle down.'

'Do you have children?'

'A boy.'

'He goes to boarding school?'

'Did Singel tell you that?'

'No, but it's obvious.'

'He would never have understood my relationship with Julio. In fact, it was Julio who was most against him being sent away to school, but that was the only way. This is a small apartment.'

'Will the boy come back to live with you now?'

'I've got used to this way of life. So has he. He's very happy as he is. Besides, I'm still young.'

'Did Julio ever write to you about anything specific in Spain? About people he knew?'

'No, he tried to avoid it. The letters he wrote were very sincere: he would tell me when he met other women, but never said who they were.'

'Had he been writing to you recently?'

'Less.'

'Have you kept his letters?'

'Some of them perhaps. At first I kept them all, but then I grew scared my son might find them. He spends the weekends with me, and they were very intimate letters.'

'Can I read them?'

'I'm sorry, but they're personal.'

'Are there any that might give me some clue as to what he was doing in Spain, where he was, who he was seeing?'

'He never mentioned any names.'

'But if he wrote to you about the women in his life, he must have said something specific about them.'

'No. Never. He had grown used to being careful.'

'No addresses either?'

'Yes, he did give those.'

She got up and rummaged in the desk drawers. She took out an envelope and handed it to Carvalho. The handwriting was laborious, as though it had been carefully studied at school, although the neatness of the strokes was spoilt by the use of a cheap biro. Carvalho looked at the sender's address on the back, and noted it down: 'Teresa Marsé, 46 Avenida General Mitre, Barcelona'.

'What links did he have with the organisation from Spain?'

'I can't answer that.'

'I mean personal links, not business ones. Did Singel and the others still feel they could trust him?'

'Completely. When he heard Julio was dead, Singel was really upset. Such a horrible death!'

The tears began to flow again. She peered at Pepe through the waterfall.

'Did you see the body?' she asked.

'No.'

'Is it true he had no face left?'

'So I heard.'

'Well then, it might not be him. Has the body's identity been confirmed?'

It's easy enough to do a tattoo. A dead body can be switched. It could well not have been Julio Chesma. In his mind's eye Carvalho no longer saw the limp, tear-stained widow, but Señor Ramón. What was he trying to confirm? The identity of a dead man, or the confirmation of an identity?

'So Julio never gave you any idea of what he was up to in Barcelona?'

'Don't start that again. You know I can't tell you anything about that. Besides, I haven't the faintest idea. I know nothing.'

'His death could have been a settling of accounts.'

'Singel thought the same and is very worried.'

The widow had got up from the bed. She was not a limp rag doll any more. She glanced at her watch: Carvalho had been told it was time to go in many less polite ways.

'I have to go,' he said, making as if to set off downstairs.

'Have you found out all you wanted to know?'

'Not everything. But the circle is closing.'

'And where is it taking you?'

'Back to the beginning. That's the surprise you get when things come full circle.'

He led the way down the stairs because he had learnt that is it polite to go upstairs behind women and to go down in front of them. Not all women understood why this was how it should be, and on more than one occasion Carvalho had seen his efforts at politeness interpreted in quite the wrong way. But the widow Salomons was well educated; she even smiled when Carvalho started down the steps ahead of her. Pepe was wondering whether he should throw a lifeline, to make their meeting into something more than a wake for a lost lover. All he had to say was: 'I'm sorry we had to meet in such tragic circumstances. Are you doing anything this evening?' By the time this thought had been transferred from brain to face, he had turned to the widow and was leering at her like a professional undertaker enquiring whether she had found the ceremony to her satisfaction.

'I'm sorry you had to go through this difficult moment. Some things are best forgotten.'

The widow Salomons' head dropped to her ample chest. Carvalho feared more waterworks. But then she lifted her head again and smiled at him through her tears with the stoic look of a Trojan woman accepting her destiny and death. Carvalho cast a last backward glance at this suffering Trojan determined despite everything to seek new lovers she could regenerate through culture. Hypersensitive lovers who deserved to be more than they were; lovers who fought the good fight in bed and kept her feeling young as long as her skin was smooth and her flesh was firm.

The desk sergeant said he did not know whether Kayser was in the building. A minute later, the big blond inspector who had visited Carvalho twice at his hotel came into the room. Kayser was in, and would not be long. The inspector again offered Carvalho one of his small cheroots. Usually Carvalho smoked only heavyweight cigars, but he took one because novelties always fascinated him.

'Have you got something interesting for Kayser?'

'My farewell. I'm leaving tomorrow morning.'

'That is interesting. We've been very worried about you, Mr Carvalho.'

'You shouldn't have worried. I'm only here as a tourist.'

'I see your eye is a lot better. There were two more attacks in the red light district last night.'

'It seems such a peaceful place.'

'Appearances can be deceptive.'

The glass door opened. An arm appeared, and then a man as massive as the blond inspector came into the office. His hair was grey, but he had such an air of energy about him that he immediately dominated the room, like one of those charismatic actors who drive everyone else off the stage. As soon as Kayser walked in, Carvalho forgot about the other man. He hardly even realised the inspector was still in the room, sitting in a corner as though he were in the front stalls to watch the show of fake conviviality Kayser and Carvalho were putting on.

'I would never have forgiven you if you'd left without saying goodbye. Even if only for old time's sake. I've heard from Inspector Israel here that you don't work for the Americans any more. You're on your own. Is it profitable?'

'Every Spaniard dreams of setting up on his own. Let's just say I work the way I want. My only responsibility is to my client.'

'I think you're wasting your talent. I've thought a lot about this, Carvalho, my friend, and it seems to me that if you stayed on here in Amsterdam you could be very useful to us. People still think highly of you, and there are lots of youngsters here who learnt all they know from you.'

'That's nice to know.'

'But this time it would be different. Have you any idea how many Spanish workers there are in Holland? More than twenty thousand. Our aim is to make their stay here as trouble free as possible, but it's not always easy. They have a different mentality. We don't see things the same way. You could ask to have a team of your own – an unofficial one, of course – and use it to keep a quiet eye on your compatriots. To protect them. They don't always make the transition successfully from such a protectionist society as yours to our permissive one. Yes, we live in a permissive society, as the sociologists call it these days, Mr Carvalho. Have you given up sociology for good?'

'I live off it.'

'Is that metaphorically speaking?'

'It could be. What do you think?'

'It's a metaphor. And a very appropriate one. What is a policeman if not a sociologist?'

Inspector Israel agreed. He stepped into the footlights for his moment of fame.

'That's true. A sociologist and a psychologist.'

'You see? Well, a permissive society like ours is bound to cause some mental confusion in your compatriots. They suddenly find they have sex and politics within easy reach.'

'But sex is expensive for all immigrants.'

'Exactly right. It's within their reach, but they can't always get their hands on it. That creates a great sense of frustration, which unfortunately it is not our job to resolve. And then there's the political question. You know that here in Holland we are extremely tolerant towards any attitude that does not directly go against our constitution. We even have Trotskyists here, Mr Carvalho. But a Dutch Trotskyist has the immense advantage of being born in Holland. So first and foremost he is a Dutchman, and his Trotskyist behaviour will not go beyond acceptable limits. But can you imagine a Spanish Trotskyist, anarchist or even a communist in Holland? Can you imagine him trying to convert his politically starved comrades? We have to keep a much closer eye on every Spanish, Greek or Turkish activist than we do on a hundred Dutchmen. It would make a fascinating job for you. Above all, classifying the different ideologies and tendencies. Assessing how important they are: that way we would know exactly how your compatriots are evolving politically. Once we knew that, we could make sure they were pointed in the right direction, and that they came to no harm by doing things that were against the grain.'

Carvalho mechanically accepted the second cheroot Israel was offering him over his shoulder. Kayser was still talking, but Carvalho had succeeded in blocking him out mentally and was thinking of other things based on what the inspector had already said. Then he realised Kayser had come to a halt and was waiting with an expectant smile for his response.

'No. It doesn't interest me. I prefer to work for myself. I'm hired to follow a woman cheating on her husband, or to find a missing relative. Or to get proof that a business associate is involved in double dealing. All nice and peaceful. I wouldn't change it for any big, transcendental stuff like ideas or politics. They require either a laudable curiosity for new techniques or an authentic ideological position. I don't have either of those any more. I work enough to live. I'm not interested in the technological advances of the profession. I don't even read about them. I've changed a lot. As for politics, I couldn't give a damn about Trotskyism or anarchism or communism, or the permissive society for that matter. I'm not even neutral. I'm aseptic.'

'You're making a big mistake. We're not trying to strangle your compatriots' new-found political freedom, merely to point it in the right direction.'

'You can strangle it or point it wherever you like, but don't count on me. I quit the CIA when I had a brilliant career ahead of me. I'd done three tours of duty, and was in line for a very important post in Colombia. But I said no, and left. I had a grand time, but I hadn't saved a cent. Now I'm putting a bit by each month because I'm nearly forty and you have to start thinking about your old age.'

Kayser laughed almost sincerely.

'It's a big mistake, I'm telling you. Somebody has to do this job, and there aren't many who have your talent or knowledge. You know the difference between a mere policeman and one who can link theory and practice. Someone who can do that is a real professional. A humanist. The others just blunder about. Do you want your compatriots to have to deal with that kind of person?'

'I don't have any compatriots. I don't even have a cat.'

Kayser laughed once again. He had stood up, and so had Israel. Carvalho got the message. Kayser was showing him out down the corridor when all of a sudden he slapped himself on the forehead and took Carvalho to one side.

'I forgot to ask how you are feeling. Inspector Israel told me about your unfortunate incident. As you see, we haven't asked you any embarrassing questions. We've respected our old friendship. But it won't be like that a second time.'

Kayser was still smiling affably.

'I trust you understand,' he went on. 'You could have died in the canal, and then we would have had a lot of explaining to do to our bosses.'

'I'm here as a tourist.'

They carried on towards the exit.

'We're all just passing through, my friend.'

Carvalho shook hands with him and Israel, then rushed out of the police station. He was in a hurry to take advantage of the remaining daylight to revisit all the hidden corners and sensations that Amsterdam had to offer, exactly like a tourist returning somewhere he once thought he knew.

Carvalho's neighbour on the plane did not want to talk. Because of everything that had happened in such a short space of time, Carvalho felt tired and so spent the flight dozing and reflecting. As soon as the plane landed at Barcelona airport he knew what he had to do. This was Charo's busiest time of day, so it was not a good idea to call her. But if she was busy with a client she would have taken her phone off the hook, so he called anyway. He was lucky. Charo herself answered.

'It's me. I need you to come up to my place tonight. It doesn't matter what time. I can't come down to you.'

'It's not exactly convenient.'

'I'll expect you. I've brought you something.'

'What is it?'

'Come and you'll see.'

He had left his car in the airport car park. He had been away for only three days, but it felt like an eternity. His car was the first friendly thing he came into contact with, and he was surprised to find he felt tender even towards a machine. As he drove across the city towards Tibidabo his capacity for surprise gradually diminished. The sights around him clung to his body like an old, well-worn garment, so that it was not long before he found himself completely at home. His letterbox was full of junk mail. He left it there to enjoy the evening breeze. He felt an urgent need to relax and light a fire. He opened the windows wide so that the cool July night air would compensate for the heat from the fire. Once again he had the problem of finding paper to light the fire with. He still had the copy of *Suck* carefully folded in his inside pocket, but he did not want to sacrifice that after all the effort he had gone to, smuggling it through Spanish customs. He preferred to burn a book, and this time he headed straight for a copy of *Don Quijote*. It was a work he had always detested, and he felt a thrill of pleasure at the mere thought of consigning it to the flames. His only regret, quickly pushed out of his mind, were the illustrations that accompanied the adventures of that idiot from La Mancha.

Taking off his jacket, he built an elaborate tepee of kindling and logs, then pushed the open *Don Quijote* underneath and lit its pages. The scene reminded him of an old story by Hans Christian Andersen in which the anxious reader follows the evolution of a flax flower from birth to death as part of a book that is burnt in a jolly Christmas fire. Carvalho still had three thousand five hundred books on the shelves enclosing his living room like the bars of a cage. Enough for daily fires for another ten years.

He took Charo's Chinese jacket out of his bag and draped it over an armchair. In the refrigerator he found dried cod, tins of beans, peppers and tomatoes, as well as some salted pork chops. He could make the special rice and cod dish that Charo liked so much. He found some Mallorcan sausage in his meat tray. A slice or two of that would go nicely with the other ingredients. He also had some beer in the cellar, and just in case had bought four cans of Dutch beer at Amsterdam airport. He got them out, along with the smoked salmon he had found at half the price he would have paid in Spain. He prepared canapés as starters. He chopped up onion, cucumber and capers. He made a paste from this and a wedge of butter, then spread it on slices of black bread. He cut slices of salmon and laid them on top.

He heard Charo's car drawing up outside as he was busy laying a damp cloth on top of the stove. He put the boiled rice on it so that the cloth would prevent any grains of rice sticking to the bottom of the pan as it settled. Charo found him drying his hands on a kitchen towel.

'What a surprise. Cooking. And a fire in the hearth. Anyone who saw a fire blazing like that in July…'

'I think it's a good idea.'

'So you want to spend the night thinking? Is that why you asked me here?'

Carvalho sensed an erotic overtone behind Charo's initial gruffness.

'I've made you rice with cod.'

'That's more like it. Oh, did you buy yourself that?' said Charo, pointing admiringly at the Chinese jacket.

'It's not for me.'

Charo had picked it up and was holding it against herself.

'Is it for me?'

'Who else?'

'Thanks, you're a sweetheart.'

She gave him two loud smacking kisses full on his lips.

Carvalho could hear the erotic drumbeat starting up, but a calmer part of his brain weighed up the disastrous consequences for his rice if he let passion take over and postpone the dinner. They would simply have to eat quickly.

Charo, who by now was wearing nothing more than the Chinese jacket, declared herself delighted with the meal.

'Is the jacket from Peking?'

'Look at the label.'

'OK, but is it really Chinese?'

'From Hong Kong.'

'Yes, that's what it says.'

Charo always wolfed down food like a growing adolescent. It was one of the things Carvalho most liked about her. He knew that nobody who is indifferent to food is to be trusted. Charo somehow sensed the exact moment to stop eating and start lovemaking. Carvalho even felt rather in love with her, perhaps because he knew what the outcome would be, and was not faced with all the problems of satisfying his desire in journeys to cities that never delivered.

They collapsed on to the floor in front of the fire. Carvalho quickly answered Charo's questions about Holland. He knew he had to if he was to be able to ask her all that he wanted to.

'What happened to your eye? It looks like someone scratched you.'

'It was a punch.'

'It looks like a scratch.'

'How have things been here?'

'Even worse. They've shut absolutely everything. Brothels,

bars, everything. Hundreds of girls are in La Trinidad jail, and they've taken more to Alcalà de Henares. Lots of other people have been arrested.'

'Are your friends still staying with you?'

'Only the girl from Andalusia. The other one was upset at what you did to her boyfriend and has gone somewhere else. Watch out for that kid. He's not really bad, but he's out for revenge.'

'Did you find Frenchy?'

'She was one of the first they put inside. Even before the raids started.'

'I need you to do me a favour. Well, not you exactly. Your friend. If you went they would recognise you and could be suspicious. Do you have your hair cut at Queta's?'

'Me, go there? You must be joking. They leave your hair like rats' tails. I go to a decent hairdresser. One on the Avenida Mistral, not one of your A-list celebrities, but someone serious. See how pretty it looks.'

'Pretty as a picture.'

'No, take a good look. Look how well it's layered. Do you think Queta could layer it like that?'

'Lovely. Listen, I need your friend to go to Queta's and take a look round. That's all. She should observe what goes on. Who comes in. Who goes out. What Queta says. What she does. And Fat Nuria. What does she get up to? And Señor Ramón. What do they say in the neighbourhood about him and Queta?'

'Not a lot. That's odd in itself. He's regarded as a real gent. They say he was married and came from a good family, but that he threw it all up for Queta when he was already well into middle age. But I haven't heard anything about whether they get on or not.'

'I want your Andalusian friend to tell me everything she sees. I don't want her to ask any questions, just to keep her eyes peeled and tell me. Well, there is one thing. She could ask what hours the girls there work and where they live.'

The caretaker told him that Señorita Marsé would not be back until six o'clock that evening. He would be sure to find her then because her boy would have been brought back on the school bus and she was always there to meet him, give him a bath and dinner, all that kind of thing. The boy, the caretaker went on unprompted, so that Carvalho would get a proper picture, spent the weekends with his father and his paternal grandparents. The other five days he lived with his mother. But if it was really urgent and he needed to get in touch with Señorita Marsé before then, she would be in her shop. A boutique in Calle Ganduxer. No more than a block farther up. The boutique, the caretaker explained so that Carvalho would not get the wrong idea, was already hers when she lived with her husband. Her husband's family was well off, but so was hers. Although not quite as rich.

Carvalho had no further need of her, so he said goodbye quite brusquely.

'Are you from social services? She's an excellent mother. The boy has everything he could possibly want. He adores her!'

'No, I'm not from social services.'

The shop was called Trip. The decor was a heady mix of modern, Moroccan and Nepalese. It would have been exactly right for that kind of area in a city such as Strasbourg. In this quiet island of a broad, clean Barcelona street, where gardens had survived all the building frenzy, Trip fulfilled its function of disguising an indeterminate number of middle-class women. It offered them a fleeting new skin, a change of decor in the cages of their bourgeois souls usually dominated by the straight lines and pure white of functionalism. Instead, it allowed them to adopt the colours and textures of a more exotic world. At the very least, Trip gave its bourgeois customers the chance to feel they were the equal of their peer group in Strasbourg and close, oh so close! to those who lived in Paris, London or San Francisco.

Teresa Marsé was wearing one of her own disguises. The apparent attack of measles disfiguring her face turned out to be a careful scattering of artificial freckles. Over a blue-eyed baby-doll face burned the slow flame of the inevitable blonde Angela Davis wig. Her body's invisible charms were covered by a bluish viscose tunic made in Marrakesh. She demonstrated that geisha-like submission so typical of those liberated young middle-class women who invested their pre-nuptial enthusiasm in these consolation prizes for unfulfilled ambitions. The ancestral tradition of setting up a girl who had brought shame to her family in a corner shop had been modified to leasing a boutique for unhappily married women suffering from existential angst. Teresa Marsé had been lucky enough to find a husband who understood this. Carvalho immediately saw that this geisha in a djellaba seemed quite level headed, and decided to dive straight in.

'I'm looking for someone called Julio Chesma. A common acquaintance in Amsterdam suggested I might try here.'

The baby-doll look was immediately wiped from Teresa Marsé's face, to be replaced by one of anguished doubt. Where was Julio? She had not heard any news of him for a couple of weeks. He had gone missing for longer before, but he always called.

'I know less than you. I need to find him urgently. I've just got here from Amsterdam and have to talk to him. There's a problem. You know what I mean.'

'No, what do you mean?'

'Have you no idea what Julio does for a living?'

'He imports Edam cheese.'

The verbal blow hit Carvalho somewhere in the pit of his soul. As he tried as hard as he could not to laugh, his face took on an ambiguous expression. Teresa Marsé scrutinised him and decided it meant bad news.

'Something's happened to Julio,' she said.

Carvalho chose a limited sincerity.

'I think you could help me if you know anything about it. But perhaps this isn't the proper place. Should we have lunch together?'

'I'm supposed to see someone. But I'll put that off. It will have to be somewhere close. I have to do some fittings this afternoon, and I need to be home by six. So let's make it somewhere where we can eat any old thing.'

That was exactly what Carvalho never wanted to eat, but he adopted all the resigned dignity of a true Galician and they agreed to meet a couple of hours later in a café on Calle Muntaner. Opposite the Boccaccio, Teresa Marsé explained, to make it absolutely clear. Carvalho decided to make the best of a bad job: he knew that at least Boccaccio was a superb Italian delicatessen. He could choose himself a delicious dinner that would make up for the horror of 'any old thing'. He walked uphill and stood gazing with pleasure at the fresh pasta laid out in the window. He did not know whether to have fettuccini or cappelletti. Once inside the shop he let several women obviously in a hurry get served in front of him. He looked along the shelves of wine for a bottle of Marcelli, found one, and then his eyes plunged into the soft mounds of cappelletti. He had made his choice, but still ran his eyes over the Parma ham, the balls of mozzarella, the jars of sauce. He already knew what the menu would be, and asked for all the ingredients without hesitation.

The imagined delights of a forthcoming dinner often came to Carvalho's aid to help him through the next few hours. Just as he had feared, Teresa Marsé turned out to have a complete lack of interest in food. She belonged to that social class which is tired of duck with orange by the age of ten, and has drunk so much good wine that they see no difference between a bottle of house red and a 1948 Chateau Laffitte. Only such tired palates could choose the kind of café food she ate: tinned artichokes with grilled chicken and chips. Carvalho tried in vain to lead by example, and opted for a simple plate of eggs and bacon, but with the eggs properly fried: none of your rubbish cooked on a hotplate, he warned the waiter, because if you do I'll wrap them round your head. He insisted they change the bottle of house red for a Paternina 1968, the only vintage on offer which succeeded in combining a reasonable price with reasonable levels of chemicals.

Teresa was observing his struggle to preserve some gastronomic pride with an irritating air of superiority. She barely picked at her food, and left half the plastic chicken and all the chips.

'Are you on a diet?'

'No, sometimes I eat like a horse. I buy myself two kilos of peaches and don't stop till I've finished them.'

'That's healthy food at least.'

Over her cup of black coffee with no sugar, Teresa returned to their main topic of conversation. In that at least she shared Carvalho's tastes. She had always suspected that Julio was mixed up in something. The fact that he used her address for his mail, for example. Carvalho explained exactly what he was mixed up in.

'Why didn't he tell me? I wouldn't have minded. I don't get it. Are you sure you don't know anything more? Has something happened to him?'

'Something could happen to him. We need to find him at once.'

'I can't help you, I'm afraid.'

'Where did he live in Barcelona?'

'No idea.'

'I don't believe you. You must have seen him somewhere, and it wouldn't have been at your place.'

'Why not there?'

'Because you wouldn't risk the scandal. I suppose your husband is a tolerant man, but not to the extent of wanting to see you receive lovers in the same apartment where his son lives.'

'How do you know all this?'

'Julio told me.'

'That's not true. It was the caretaker. I called her and she told me everything. She thought she was doing me a favour because you were a spy from my husband.'

'Fine, let's forget about that. Where did you two meet?'

'My parents have a house they no longer use. Quite close to here: at Caldetas, by the seaside.'

'I know where Caldetas is.'

'We used to go there. My parents never visit it. They keep saying they're going to sell it, but can never make up their minds. I think they've even forgotten they still have it. We used to meet there. That way we didn't have to go to my apartment or to Julio's.'

'Did you ever meet any of his friends? Do you know what he got up to? Did he often go somewhere? Where did he eat?'

'When we ate together we used to come here. I don't know anything more about his life.'

'How did you meet?'

'It's a long story.'

'I have the time.'

'I don't.'

But she found time from somewhere. They crossed the street to the Oxford. It was a showy, empty place which made it perfect to talk in. Between the waiters and the tables was a loud wall of customers enjoying a late aperitif at the bar. Teresa told Carvalho how she had met Julio in the office of an importer of Dutch products. She had gone to pick up her order of Indonesian knick-knacks and Amsterdam hippy creations. Julio was there enquiring about a load of Edam cheese. As she said this, Teresa burst out laughing. Carvalho joined in, relieved he did not have to suppress his mirth as he had done the first time he heard such an unlikely story.

'Julio made fun of some of the things I was buying. I did the same. Then he started on my clothes, and I replied in kind. I said he dressed like a country bumpkin from Vitoria dazzled by big-city executives. I knew he was trying to pick me up, but I liked the look of him and I thought it might be worthwhile finding out whether there was anything more to him. And there was. He had class.'

She was talking about her past with Chesma in a way that Carvalho thought was too flippant. She was aware it had all been a game. She was not as emotionally involved as the widow Salomons had been. Teresa Marsé went through life willing to be surprised, but in fact was not often caught unawares. Julio Chesma offered her the novelty of someone she could not easily categorise. A rough-and-ready sort who knew how to disguise the fact. A man with no education who had taught himself a lot. A man of imagination with hands strong enough to get a good grasp on reality.

'We didn't have what you might call a steady relationship. I made things very clear to him from the outset: I hadn't got free of the marriage yoke just to imprison myself again. At first he didn't understand. I think jealousy was one of his many contradictions. He was terribly jealous. Just the thought that I might go out with other men drove him crazy.'

'Did you take them to the same place in Caldetas?'

'Why not? Julio himself used to go there with other women. After I had managed to convince him we shouldn't be each other's jailer, he asked me several times if he could use the house. I knew what it was for, and gave him the key. Would you like it?'

'Would you come with me?'

Teresa Marsé weighed Carvalho up with a sceptical smile.

'It's a possibility. But at the moment I'm in the midst of a passionate affair.'

'With Julio?'

'No, that's almost completely finished with. By the way, what time is it?'

'How come a woman as busy as you doesn't wear a watch?'

'It leaves a mark on your wrist. And besides, I think it's a stupid habit.'

'But you must be glad that others have them…'

'Yes, that's true.'

Carvalho followed her out. As she had done in the café, Teresa let him pay.

'Stop by the shop another day and I'll treat you, OK?'

'Which day?'

'Don't harass me.'

'Not my style. I just want you to tell me the day and time of our next rendez-vous.'

'Don't be so sensitive! Give me a call. That's the best way.'

She took a business card with the boutique details on it from her seemingly bottomless embroidered bag. Carvalho put it in his pocket, then did something he hardly ever did: he gave her his address in Vallvidrera.

'So you don't need to take anyone to your parents' place. Is it your house or your bachelor pad?'

'Both.'

'Men! You always get away with things we women never can.'

They were walking along a side street that came out almost exactly level with her boutique in Calle Ganduxer.

'Julio used to get letters from an old flame in Amsterdam, didn't he?'

'Yes, he did. The widow Salomons. He read me one once.'

She raised her hand to her face and giggled. Then she went on: 'You should have heard it! She even quoted Catullus at him! That gives you some idea of what it was like. Julio was very grateful to her because she helped him educate himself. He was very quick, very receptive. I used to leave him books and he would return them with whole passages underlined. He was what you might call "a mind wasted from lack of opportunities". But he was doing well in life. He was earning a lot more than many non-wasted minds. It's all relative, isn't it? He made a lot of money, or at least he seemed to. He always had a lot on him, and was always well dressed. Too well dressed. There was nothing I could do about it: he had an almost religious respect for made-to-measure suits, shiny shoes, slick ties and so on.'

'He was born to raise hell in hell.'

'So you know about the tattoo? He told me he had always been a rebel. As a kid in the orphanage, in the Spanish Legion, and then in jail. Did you know he'd been in jail? A priest told him in the orphanage one day: "You're worse than the devil." Julio told everyone that. It used to amuse him, because in recent months he was living like a lord, he had a happy, settled existence and yet he still had that tattoo.'

'Perhaps it was his way of making sure he hung on to that part of himself.'

'Could be. Give me a call one of these days.'

With that she vanished inside her shop of disguises.

No. She was not the sort of woman who waited in weary bars for the return of a young sailor with a heart tattooed on his chest. Carvalho was sure that such a woman existed in Julio Chesma's life, but that neither the theatrical and literary widow Salomons nor the playful Teresa Marsé were her. Somewhere, although he did not know where, before or after Chesma had begun his journey towards a faceless death, a woman had been marked for ever by his vitality and strength. Carvalho had no idea if he was so convinced of this because of the song, or if it was thanks to his own instinct. A man like Julio Chesma could never have been satisfied with a melodramatic widow or a tennis partner like Teresa Marsé. He needed someone who could identify completely with his tattoo's message. The tattoo was aimed at someone who had taken Julio Chesma's life as seriously as her own.

He arranged to meet Charo and her friend from Andalusia at a restaurant in San Cugat. It was quite close for Carvalho, but Charo was as mad as hell when she arrived.

'I don't understand why you can't come down to my place. Why are you playing this game of hide-and-seek?'

Her friend tried to soothe her.

'He knows what's he's doing.'

'You could at least have made us dinner at your place.'

'I bought things for dinner but I wasn't in the mood to make it. There's a time for everything. Perhaps I'll cook anyway, and have a late supper.'

Charo turned to the Andalusian as though she had caught Pepe red handed.

'See? And he's serious. Can you believe it? He's capable of starting to cook at four in the morning.'

Charo was looking at Carvalho the way a mother looks at a beloved child unfortunately born with two heads. Her friend laughed so much Carvalho could see her two gold back teeth.

'I just love this place,' she said, like an actress from a Spanish soap opera.

Carvalho was not so sure, especially as it was decorated like the Escorial Palace, with period furniture made in the neighbourhood. He was unsure about its specialities as well: bread smeared with tomato, sausage and beans, barbecued meat, or rabbit with alioli sauce. In the previous decade something like ten thousand restaurants had opened in Catalonia purporting to offer their customers the marvels of simple rustic Catalan cooking. But far too often, their bread with tomato (an imaginative creation far superior to pizza with tomato) was little more than a lump of humid, undercooked dough made even more soggy by a layer of tinned tomato puree. And the alioli sauce had usually not been prepared with enough patience and had the egg yolk added as if it were mayonnaise, with the result that it looked like yellow house paint. Carvalho found himself giving the astounded ladies a lecture on the gastronomic roots of humanity. But it wasn't so much Charo's friend's exclamation 'My God, what a lot this guy knows' which made him wonder about what he was doing talking like this, as the moment when he heard himself utter the word 'matrix' to describe the common origin of some dishes.

'Just as we can speak of a linguistic matrix and can situate the common source of Aryan languages in Indo-European, so we can trace a gastronomic matrix, one of whose manifestations is the combination of bread with tomato. This is obviously related to pizza, but is even easier to prepare. Pizza dough has to be cooked, whereas bread with tomato is simply that: bread and tomato with a little salt and oil sprinkled on it.'

'And it's really delicious,' said the Andalusian girl, full of enthusiasm for all the mysteries Carvalho was revealing to her. 'It's refreshing and filling. And it has a lot of goodness in it. Dr Cardelús told me so when I took my boy to see him because he was a bit anaemic. Give him *bones llesques* of bread with *tomàquet y pernil,* he said. It worked like a charm. My boy is in a house in the country near Gavá. And I always tell the people looking after him to give him bread and tomato, heaps of it.'

Carvalho was worried that the scientific tone of the debate had languished somewhat, but at that moment the famous bread with tomato arrived. It was not of a quality to figure in the best cookbooks, but it was proper bread and tomato. The two women waited expectantly for Carvalho's verdict. He rolled it around the roof of his mouth, trying to decide how fresh the bread was, if the tomato was firm, and to judge the quality of the oil.

'They've used slightly damp salt, but it'll do.'

'My God, is there nothing he doesn't know?'

Charo already knew all Carvalho's party tricks and was not yet ready to forgive him for having made them travel so far. She grunted.

'Well, I like it,' she said. 'Besides, I'm hungry. You're too finicky, Pepe. It's obvious you've never been really hungry in your life.'

'Yes, it's dreadful to go hungry,' her Andalusian friend agreed. She was determined to have her say about anything the other two mentioned. Her thin lips were smothered in oil, and Carvalho was pleased to see her make short work of the barbecued ribs. They were served a bottle of rosé. Pepe thought it quite sweet, with an interesting aftertaste, so he asked where it came from.

'It tastes to me like a wine from the Ampurdán, somewhere around Perelada or Corbella.'

'You're almost there. We have it brought from up above Montmany.'

'It's not bad at all.'

'It goes down well. It's not too strong, but very pleasant.'

'Not strong?' the Andalusian girl was doing her Jerry Lewis impression. 'Not strong?'

Her eyes had crossed.

'It's already gone straight to my head.'

She straightened her eyes again and roared with laughter at her own joke, all the while picking shreds of meat from between her teeth with a toothpick.

'Never mind that, tell him how you got on this morning.'

'Oh yes, Pepe, I had a real laugh. You don't need an assistant more often, do you?'

She lowered her voice to a stage whisper.

'I was spying on them the whole morning. Look at what they did to my hair. Not bad, is it? I thought it was going to be worse. I got them to do the whole works: I was in there from nine in the morning till two this afternoon.'

'So?'

'So what?'

'So what did you find out?'

'They're very busy. Very. The four girls and Queta can hardly cope. If only I'd listened to my mother! You know, Pepe, I'm from Bilbao really, but in our line of business you have to say you're Andalusian if you want to keep the client happy. I've no idea why. So I soon started speaking with an accent and swaying my hips like a flamenco dancer, and now I half believe I'm from Seville myself.'

Carvalho had always thought that prostitutes from the Basque country, Catalonia or even Madrid pretended they were Andalusians out of pure racism. They transferred their shame about how they earned their living on to Spain's least developed region, in this way somehow preserving the ethnic purity of the Basques, the noble lineage of Castille, and Catalan industrial prowess. But Charo's friend insisted it was all down to the clients.

'It's what they want. If you tell them you're from Bilbao they look at you disappointed. As if you're not going to give them a good time.'

It was her turn to give them a lecture. She demonstrated that even in whoring theory is the inseparable companion of practice, and that the division of labour has produced disasters splitting the two apart not only in almost every area of art and the professions, but also in philosophy, sociology and even whorology. The authors of the vast majority of books written about prostitution are therapists who know nothing about what really goes on, and the Basque-Andalusian girl's critical capacities knocked all their theories into a cocked hat.

'As soon as they see a client, lots of the girls start with their Andalusian lovey-dovey stuff and lisping about what a good time they're going to give them. Some clients like it, but there are others who don't. It all depends.'

Carvalho tried to bring her spaceship back into the earth's atmosphere, and in particular to Queta's hair salon.

'Oh yes, that. They work so hard! It reminded me of my poor mother who wanted me to be a hairdresser. If I had listened to her by now I'd be set up for life and earning a fortune.'

'You're not doing so badly. You can't complain.'

'This isn't the moment to tell me that, Pepe. I've been in hiding for more than a week and haven't earned a cent. Not like your friend here. She's been clever, thanks to you. There's not many men who would have done what you did for Charo, Pepe. A lot of them would have just exploited her. You told her to choose her clients carefully and to wait for them to come to her. Not to go out on to the streets looking for them. She's almost respectable.'

Eyes moist with tears, Charo put her hand on Pepe's and squeezed it affectionately. One day I'll marry her, he thought. The wine really must be stronger than it seemed. He would marry Charo, but only when they were old and grey.

'Very old,' he blurted out without meaning to.

After two coffees each they returned to business. It was a warm, star-filled night. They went out into the square opposite San Cugat monastery, and strolled along while the Andalusian girl told them what she had seen. Carvalho was walking in shirtsleeves between the two women, his arms round their shoulders.

'There are four girls as well as Queta. Her husband is always in the upstairs office, except when he comes down and goes for a drink in the bar on the corner. Otherwise he gets Fat Nuria to bring him something. The four assistants are very young and friendly. Fat Nuria is the most recent, but she's almost more in charge than Queta. She's very full of herself. The others start at nine in the morning and have no fixed time to leave. Well, they've all gone by nine in the evening, except on Saturdays when they can be there as late as ten, working behind closed doors. Two of the girls live together. They're sisters, from Andalusia. Real Andalusians, Pepe. They're hard workers: they started in Jaén. And Queta shows a lot of patience training them. They're not very talented, but they're learning. The third assistant has a proper fiancé. He comes to meet her every day from work, even though sometimes he has to wait for hours in the bar for her to finish. She's Catalan, from Barceloneta. Her father and brothers work in the port. Fat Nuria is the only one who has lunch in the salon because she does the shopping for Queta, and often buys the food. She always leaves at eight because she lives in Badalona and her brother comes for her in a delivery van.'

'Is he a driver, then?'

'No, it's his own van. The family has a salted and frozen fish business down by the shore at Badalona. Fat Nuria's father used to be a ship's carpenter, but he had a bad problem with his eyes. He couldn't stand the paint, the sawdust or anything else in the carpentry shop. Strange, isn't it? The smell of fish from the warehouse doesn't affect him in the least.'

'How do the girls get on with Queta?'

'Well, there's a bit of friction with Fat Nuria, because she's so full of herself. The boss thinks the world of her. You can tell because sometimes he asks for things it would be easier for Queta to bring, but that minx always gets in first. Queta doesn't like that, it's obvious.'

She tapped her nostril.

'But she's a pussycat really. She's so fat you think she could eat everything in sight, but she's not so bad underneath.'

'What's Queta like physically?'

'Don't tell him, you'll only arouse his imagination.'

'Aren't the two of us enough for you, Pepe, darling?'

'What do you mean, "the two of us"? I'm his girlfriend, remember.'

Pepe squeezed the two hens' necks and prevented them taking it any farther.

'What do they say about Señor Ramón and Queta?'

'Well, apparently he was happily married. He has grown-up children with his wife. Queta was her manicurist, and he fell for her. Things became serious, and in the end he left his wife and children. He set Queta up in the hair salon, and ever since he's been there too, up in the office looking after the accounts. There's no talk of either of them having anyone else. He's getting on a bit, he must be around sixty, but Queta has just turned forty and her body is still young. Weren't you asking what she was like? Well, she has a young body. She looks good for her age. She hasn't had any children or brought any up, and that shows. There's twenty years between them, and that shows too. They got together fifteen years ago, when he was in his second childhood and she was still a child. But now... a woman has her needs, don't you think?'

'Yes, you're right. What about Señor Ramón? Does he have any regular visitors?'

'Yes, there are salesmen, people selling perfumes, hair products, that kind of thing. He's in charge of all that side

of the business. They can't be doing too badly, because
Queta told me they've bought land out by Mollet. It's a very
good area because that's where they're going to put all the
factories. Which is a good idea, because factories in a city
like Barcelona only pollute the air we breathe. You almost
have to wear a gas mask as it is. Just take a breath up here.
It's wonderful. Come on, I'll buy you both an *horchata*.'

They drank it standing up next to a stall lit by a chain
of coloured lights, yellow and red streamers and blue paper
cloths. The man selling *horchata* was dressed in white and
had a navy beret on. Around his neck he wore a polka-dot
scarf. He looked the two women up and down, but when
his eyes caught Carvalho's he soon stopped his inspection.
Charo and her friend were giggling at everything, pushing
and nudging each other. Carvalho was trying to stay aloof,
enjoying the cold *horchata*, which tickled his tastebuds with
a thousand tiny pinpricks of creamy flavour.

'Listen, sweetheart. How does Fat Nuria come to have so
many privileges at the hairdresser's?'

'I don't understand.'

'How did she get to be so important there? She can't be
more than sixteen.'

'She's fifteen, but seeing she's as fat as a pig she looks
older. She's got more up here than I have,' she said, squeezing
her own breasts. 'To tell you the truth, I've no idea. I think
her father and Señor Ramón know each other. It was her
father who got her into the salon. She wants to spend three
more years there, then set up on her own in Badalona. She
knows what she wants. For example, she's got the boss to let
her have Monday afternoons off so she can go to see famous

hairdressers put on special styling shows for others in the business. That's the best way to learn. Hairdressers come from all over Catalonia, as well as apprentices and even some city officials. The two sisters asked Señor Ramón if they could do the same, even if it came out of their wages. One each on alternate Mondays. But he refused. Yet he lets Fat Nuria go. She disappears every Monday and he doesn't even take it out of her wages. I reckon Queta must be really fed up with it. I don't blame her.'

They walked back to their cars. Charo's friend insisted she lent her the car and stayed with Carvalho up in Vallvidrera.

'I'll put it in the car park and everything. Give me the keys and I'll see to it.'

'No and no. Pepe doesn't want me to stay with him, and I don't either.'

'You want her to stay, don't you, Pepe?'

Carvalho shrugged his shoulders.

'Let me have the car, Charo, then you can go with him and have another supper.'

That set them both off laughing again, but Carvalho was wondering whether he could face cooking the cappelletti at that time of night. He did not want them to dry out in his fridge, but he really did not feel like spending any time in the kitchen now.

'I'm not going to let you have the car.'

'I really don't mind taking it for you.'

'But I mind.'

'Don't you trust me to drive it safely?'

'Yes, that must be the reason.'

'Can you believe it? She lets me run amok in her

apartment and her fridge, but won't let me have her car. Charo, don't be like one of those men who won't lend you their precious fountain pen, their car or their wife.'

'Well, that's what I am like.'

'So you won't lend me your car?'

'No.'

'Your fountain pen?'

'I don't have one.'

'Pepito here?'

'Forget it.'

The Bilbao-Andalusian turned to Pepe, her eyes completely crossed.

'She's a real spoilsport, isn't she?'

Every day in the newspapers Bromuro found confirmation of his suspicions about what people were given to eat and drink. He was a stalwart champion of ecological and consumers' problems who was so ahead of his time that his views went unrecognised by theoreticians who had jumped on the bandwagon much more recently. He had already broadened his attacks far beyond what he saw as the anti-erotic plot to introduce bromide into drinking water, soft drinks bottles and mass-produced bread.

'Can't you smell it?'

'All I can smell is your polish.'

'I wish that's all it was. That's a healthy smell. I've been breathing it all my life, and I'm still alive and kicking. But is that what causes my bronchitis? Or my ulcer? Of course not. It's the air in this city. Can't you smell it? Completely polluted.'

Bromuro ended his dire pronouncement with a stealthy look all round his client in an effort to convince him that within a twenty-metre radius there were evil forces at work that could damage his body's most delicate fibres.

'Shoeshine?'

Carvalho accepted his offer. As Bromuro knelt in front of him, it was as though his voice were coming out of the top of his bald head.

'Have you got another five hundred pesetas?'

'Have you got something for me?'

'No, but I just thought that as you've been so generous lately...'

'Are you sure you haven't found out anything?'

'Nothing. There's nobody left to ask. Anyone who isn't inside has left the country. It looks as though quite a few have been rounded up. They've gone right to the top this time. Of course, nothing will happen to the big fish, but for the moment they're like rabbits in headlights: not making a move. What I can tell you is that your drowned man had a record, and a long one at that. And all the rest followed from that. Frenchy was the first to be picked up. She won't be out in a long while. The dead guy didn't say a word, but she landed everyone else in it.'

'What's this Frenchy like?'

'She's blonde. Fat, but solid. Young. A great arse. She pretended she was French. You've probably seen her street-walking on the Rambla, near Calle Fernando. Then she struck lucky and moved up to the Sarriá highway. She had lost weight recently. They like them a bit thinner up there. Like film stars, like that dry stick of a woman in *Butch Cassidy and the Sundance Kid*. Did you like her?'

Carvalho knew he had to be careful not to offend Bromuro.

'She wasn't bad.'

'But she had nothing in front and even less behind! When

that guy drew his revolver and told her to take all her clothes off, I said to myself, what, are you some kind of idiot, with a gun and a half like that you could get yourself something far juicier than her. Poor clown. I'm not saying I'd kick her out of bed: there's no woman who doesn't deserve a favour. And there's the problem: there are so many of them, and we've got so little to keep them happy with.'

'Don't get started.'

'Well, it's good to have a philosophy in life. And this is mine.'

Bromuro stood up, and took Pepe by surprise. He was tense and alert as though waiting to leap on stage for his big moment:

'The philosophy of the hand's vital triangle.'

He put his thumb down near his trouser pocket, and his little finger over his fly. Then he flicked his thumb up and down across the trouser front.

'Money, fucking and food.'

He picked up his box, pocketed Carvalho's coins and left without another word. His exit was worthy of the climax of one of Don José Ortega y Gasset's lectures. A few moments later, Carvalho got up too. A sea breeze carried the oily smell of the sea from down by Puerta de la Paz right up the Rambla. On top of his spike, Columbus was pointing unconcernedly at the noonday sky, in what seemed more like a challenge to the sun than an attempt to indicate the way to the Americas. Carvalho took off his jacket and slung it across his arm. He walked on until he came to the door of Queta's hair salon. It was open, although there were no clients inside. The sound of his footsteps on the green lino brought a question from the mezzanine office:

'Who's there?'

'It's me, Carvalho.'

It was Fat Nuria's voice. Carvalho did not wait for anyone to tell him what to do, but leapt quickly up the stairs and entered the office. All the papers had disappeared from the desk. Instead it was covered by a plastic cloth. Queta, Señor Ramón and Fat Nuria were eating Russian salad and fried fillets of fish. The two women looked down at their plates as though they were somehow trying to protect the intimacy of their meal. Señor Ramón, on the other hand, had stood up. He laid his serviette carefully on the table and said:

'Care to join us?'

'No, thanks. Sorry to have interrupted you.'

'That doesn't matter. Let's go downstairs.'

Queta glanced at Carvalho out of the corner of her eye. Fat Nuria already had her mouth full, but was busy shovelling in another fork's worth of salad. Señor Ramón emerged slowly from behind the desk and pointed the way back down the staircase. When they were in the salon, he sat in one of the metal chairs. Carvalho did the same.

'When did you get back?'

'Last night.'

'Have a good trip?'

Carvalho pointed to the scar above his eye.

'More or less.'

Señor Ramón barely glanced at the wound, but sat waiting for Carvalho to tell him his news.

'The corpse has got a name. He was called Julio Chesma. He was a drug trafficker.'

'Did he have contacts in Barcelona?'

'Yes.'

'Do you know who they were?'

'You asked me to discover the drowned man's identity. That was all.'

'Yes, that's true. My wife has a relative who's a bit wild. A real tearaway, in fact. She knew he had a tattoo with some ridiculous motto. She couldn't remember what it was exactly, but remembered it was pretty unusual. When she read the story of the drowned man in the newspaper she was very worried, so I tried to find out who he was on her behalf. She'll be very relieved, because that wasn't her relative's name.'

'Let's go and tell her, then.'

'No, let me do it. I'll find the best way. You know what women are like: they get hysterical over nothing. Now she'll be able to get on with her life. You said his name was Julio Chesma? And that it was to do with drugs? Yes, I had heard something. I knew all the raids in the days after they found the body were connected in some way. Fine. Did you discover anything more about the case? Who he had connections with, for example?'

'A few.'

'In Holland?'

'And here.'

'Who were they?'

'I don't think they'd interest you. You wanted to reassure your wife, and you can do that now.'

'But I'm curious. After all, it was me who paid for your investigation.'

'If what you want to know is whether I found any links between Julio Chesma and you, for example, the answer is no. He was a man who lived on a lot of different levels. The police have got as far as drugs. I found the same, but also a few emotional ties he had. You don't seem to be involved there either.'

'Why would I be? I never knew the man. It's all been a mistake. I'll pay you the seventy thousand: the fifty I owe you, plus expenses.'

'Correct.'

Señor Ramón clambered back up to his office. Carvalho went over to the foot of the stairs just in case he could overhear any conversation. Fat Nuria was sitting on the third step up, peeling a peach. The peel snaked downwards in one long piece to a plate she had placed on the stair between her legs. She smiled when Pepe poked his head round the corner, but he did not back away. She peered at him quizzically. Pepe stared back, looking directly at the bluish triangle of her knickers. Fat Nuria quickly snapped her legs shut, and the plate fell down the stairs. Pepe triumphantly pulled his head back. Fat Nuria muttered and bent over to pick up the remains of her peach and the plate. Señor Ramón stepped over the mess and handed Carvalho a white envelope. Pepe stuffed it in his inside pocket. He walked away without another word, but paused at the salon door. Señor Ramón and Fat Nuria were both staring at him from the foot of the stairs with a look of contained fury.

'I'm still puzzled that you should pay me so much money

to find out something you could just as easily have done yourself by walking fifty metres up the street to the nearest police station.'

'I didn't pay you to be puzzled. I found out what I wanted to know. So now goodbye and good luck.'

'I'm not so easily satisfied. I'd like to know a lot more than I do.'

He called her at six in the evening, and by eight Teresa had appeared, dressed as a rich young divorcee with leftist leanings, the sort of woman who spends summer in the city. Always a djellaba that she bought somewhere, without even realising it was a djellaba. She could just as easily have been disguised as a Touareg or a Mayan woman in the shadow of Chichen Itzá. She looked like the living symbol of liberated womanhood. She clung to Carvalho's arm, and spoke only after he had gone a hundred metres with no indication of where they were heading.

'What was your idea for tonight? Are you trying to get more information out of me, or do you want to sleep with me?'

'For the moment I want to have dinner.'

'I'll eat any old thing.'

'Well, I won't. Here: it's my first gift of the evening.'

He handed her an old book, the covers of which had faded from pink to off-yellow.

'*The Physiology of Taste*, by Savarin. What am I supposed to do with it?'

'Read it at your leisure. I bet you've read *Materialism and Empiriocriticism*, haven't you?'

'Yes, of course. A… long, long time ago.'

'Well, now read this one. That way your taste buds will be educated and you won't torture your friends by asking them to eat frozen croquettes.'

'What are you exactly? A cop? A Marxist? A gourmet?'

'I'm an ex-cop, an ex-Marxist and a gourmet.'

Carvalho took the initiative and headed for Quo Vadis. He returned the friendly greetings of the family who ran the restaurant, presided over by the impressive mother sitting in a chair anchored by the front door. When she saw the prices on the menu, Teresa immediately offered:

'I'll only have one course.'

'Are you short of money?'

'No, but I feel bad spending so much on food. I would have been happy going to a much less fancy place.'

'The thing is, I still haven't got over my lingering respect for the bourgeoisie, and I still think they know how to live.'

'Who says they don't?'

'Eighty-nine per cent of the bourgeoisie in the city dine on overcooked spinach and a tiny fish eating its own tail.'

'At least it's healthy.'

'If they added raisins and pine kernels to the spinach and ate a nice piece of dorado with herbs, wrapped in silver foil and baked in the oven, it would be just as healthy, not much more expensive, and yet much more imaginative.'

'What's so strange is that you mean it.'

'Naturally. Sex and food are the two most serious things in life.'

'That's really odd. Julio used to say something similar. Not exactly that, but similar. He also wanted to educate his palate. He wasn't as advanced as you, he was only at the stage of sole meunière or duck with orange. Typical dishes for parvenus.'

When Carvalho saw that all she was ordering was fried eggs with ham, he was tempted to throw the bottle of vodka at her. He had started with blinis soaked in chilled vodka, and was hoping for some support. He followed the first course with bull's steak fillet. Teresa could not help commenting on the mound of dark, bloody meat spilling over his plate.

'It's bad to eat all that late at night and in midsummer too.'

'At home I always have a fire going. Even in midsummer.'

Teresa giggled like a minor starlet in Hollywood films, one who had made a career of playing dippy girls who go from bar to bar in search of adventure.

'Would you like to see my home fire burning?'

'You may have a lot of imagination when it comes to food, but your pick-up line leaves a lot to be desired. What you just said sounds just like: "Would you like to come back to my place for a drink?"'

'I've got a bottle of lemonade.'

'I prefer whisky. I hope you're not going to disappoint me. Have you got Chivas?'

'Chivas and all his court.'

'Fine.'

As they headed up towards Vallvidrera, Teresa was humming 'Penny Lane'.

'If you really want to be a gourmet you have to talk differently.'

'I don't get it.'

'All the self-respecting Spanish gourmets I know have a French accent. And you have to choose French-sounding adjectives to describe things. A dish is "insuperable", or "incomparable". And you have to say them as though you were a Frenchman. Go on, say "vichyssoise".'

'Vichisois.'

'See what I mean? If you say it like that, it loses all its charm. It sounds as though it's garlic soup.'

When they arrived, she expressed her delight at everything she saw. She allowed Carvalho to light the fire in the hearth. They sat half undressed near the door, watching the flames with the cool night air from the hills on their backs but with the shifting heat from the burning wood warming their chests.

'When do you want to talk about Julio? Before or after?'

Carvalho did not want to yield an inch. He calmed his growing desire.

'Right now.'

'I think I've told you all I know.'

'The key. The key you used to leave for Julio. Who did he use it for?'

'I don't know.'

The glow from the fire decreased at that moment, or perhaps it was Teresa's face that suddenly betrayed her. As it was, Carvalho knew he should press her harder.

'Yes you do.'

'No.'

Carvalho had heard five hundred 'no's just like that during interrogations where he had been either the interrogator or the interrogated. He picked up Teresa's djellaba and threw it on the fire. She grew hysterical, rushed towards the hearth, and tried to pluck her dress out of the flames with her fingers. Furious, she turned towards him and shouted that he was a complete idiot, although this lost some of its effect because she realised how she must look: a woman in her underclothes, perspiring from the heat, caught between anger and fear. Carvalho stood up and went over to her. He grasped the back of her neck and squeezed until he was hurting her. He forced her down to the floor right next to the hearth.

'Who did he go to Caldetas with?'

His tone of voice was neutral. Teresa tried to discern menace in it, but if there was any, it was well hidden beneath what sounded like almost friendly words.

'I swear I don't know.'

'What do you know, then?'

'Let me go. I'm burning.'

Carvalho pushed her head even closer to the flames. As he increased the pressure, his voice remained calm.

'What happened in Caldetas?'

Teresa was sweating freely now. Shiny rivulets ran down her throat and across her hot breasts, which were filling the scanty bra like soft nocturnal fruits. When she spoke, her voice sounded strangled.

'If you let me go, I'll tell you.'

Carvalho helped her stand up. He put his arm round her shoulder and they walked back to the far side of the room. He stroked her cheek, and caressed the sheen of her hot nocturnal fruit.

'It was one Friday. A few weeks ago. I went to Caldetas with a friend. At first I didn't notice anything. It was he who saw something odd, and eventually we discovered that something must have happened there. There were traces of blood that had not been washed off properly. Everywhere. In the bedroom. The sink. Then outside too. In the garden there were tracks made by a big vehicle, possibly a van or small truck. That's all.'

Carvalho had learnt enough for now. His fingers did not stop at the uncovered skin. He peeled off the rest of her clothes and admired the striped golden brown and white of her body, poised between fear and desire.

He had a confused memory of having rushed Teresa back down the hill at top speed, and that when he returned he barely had time to pull back the sheets and collapse naked in bed before falling fast asleep. He woke up late and did not go down into the city until after lunch. He filled his afternoon by wandering through the old artisans' district round El Borne. The narrow streets formed a maze that was sometimes plunged into darkness, while at others the filtered rays of the sun caressed its grey stone walls. He feasted his eyes on the worn edges of the buildings, the yellow flowers poking out of any crevice where time had eroded the stone to allow their roots to take hold, the heraldic crests over huge doorways, the silence disturbed only by the cries of street traders or the throb of machines in the distance, while hidden deep in gloomy alleyways were workshops lit by twenty-five-watt bulbs so fly-speckled and covered in decades of dust they hardly give off any light at all. Cars were parked in the wider streets, but there seemed to be few going anywhere. Carvalho drank from the fountain outside Santa María del Mar church. He bought several different kinds of olives in a shop and ate them slowly with a soft bread roll he had discovered lying in solitary splendour in a basket at the first baker's to open for the afternoon. Many of the shops and workshops had heavy wooden doors with layers of faded paint and huge studs smeared with the same paint, relics of a glorious past now turned to rust. The three ages of a door and of the life of this craftsmen's neighbourhood were evident in these studs, hammered into wood that was as fibrous as stewed meat.

He went into a Galician restaurant opposite Santa María and had a bowl of broth and some slices of a soft, rather bland cheese. He could not deny that the cheeses his uncle sent him had more taste. He emerged from the backstreets into Vía Layetana. As he walked past the police headquarters he glanced at it quickly out of the corner of his eye in a way he had never tried to justify to himself: he just knew he felt uncomfortable there and always walked past as quickly as he could, as though he had suddenly thought of something he had to do.

He decided to see a film. He sat through a porno movie and then a Spanish one in which the supposed gay ends up married with five children and a wife with a face like a squashed toad. The lady with the toad features turned out to be Princess Ira von Furstenberg. When he came out of the cinema he enjoyed the feeling that he could have a cold *horchata* then start at the top of the Rambla and walk slowly down it at a time when the cool of the evening had once more filled the central avenue with passers-by and meditative souls who sat on their folding stools to watch the world go by. He hesitated over whether to buy a newspaper or a set of five lottery tickets from the blind man on the corner of Calle Buen Suceso. He chose the tickets.

After a while he made his way to the car park in Calle Pintor Fortuny. It was going to be hard to find somewhere to park close to Queta's salon, somewhere that would give him a good view of all the comings and goings. He went along Calle del Carmen out towards the Rambla again. The grey ravine of buildings ended in front of the baroque splendour of Belén church and the lively scene of the flower seller's stall in the centre of the avenue. He ventured out into the river of cars heading down to the sea. The traffic was moving so slowly he got several opportunities to ogle girls he shot past when the cars speeded up, and he felt he was spying in secret on the gathering shadows that slowly filled the street with night. The Rambla was like an entire universe that began at the port and ended at the disappointing mediocrity of Plaza Catalunya. Somehow it had retained the wise capriciousness of the rushing stream it had once been. It was like a river that knew where it was heading, like all the people walking up and down it all day long, who seemed unwilling to say goodbye to its plane trees, its multicoloured kiosks, the strange stalls selling parrots and monkeys, the archaeology of buildings which told the story of three hundred years' history of a city with a history. Carvalho loved the Rambla the way he loved his life: it was irreplaceable.

As soon as he had gone past the Liceo, he prepared to turn into the narrow streets of the Chinese quarter. The drivers behind him were so impatient he found it impossible to find anywhere to park close to Queta's salon, so he went out and round the Rambla again before plunging a second time into the array of streets rendered almost impenetrable by their narrowness and the night. This time he parked up on the pavement. It was eight in the evening by now and he reckoned it was unlikely the traffic wardens would still be as vigilant as they were during the daytime. He had a clear view of the front of the hairdresser's. The lights were on, but the blinds and photos of models in the window prevented him seeing anything inside. He switched on his radio, and almost immediately two curious passers-by were staring at him. Carvalho pushed a Bee Gees cassette into the gaping mouth of the player. They sounded to him like the apotheosis of the inability to be happy.

He had time to listen to both sides of the cassette and to light a dried-out cigar he found in his glovebox. But just as he was pushing the lighter back into its slot he saw a van pull up behind him. Nobody got out, but somebody sounded the horn three times. Shortly afterwards, the door to the hairdresser's opened and Fat Nuria came rushing out. Carvalho bent down over the gearstick. She went running past his window towards the van. Carvalho straightened up and in his rear-view mirror saw her climb inside. He let the van pull out in front of him, then switched on his ignition. He caught up with its white rear doors, and stayed on its tail. The driver was looking for a way out of the narrow streets on to the Rambla. There was less traffic now, so it was easy for Carvalho to follow him down past the monument to Columbus. Then the van headed for Plaza Palacio, turned at right angles to the other cars at Ciudadela, and continued on across Marina bridge out towards the motorway. Carvalho followed as it took the junction for Badalona.

It was more difficult to keep it in sight through the labyrinth of tiny streets leading down to the promenade in Badalona. The van parked close to some fairground stalls and a brightly lit merry-go-round from where the music of *Love Story* was blaring. Fat Nuria got out, bought an ice cream at a cart lit by a single blue bulb, then clambered back into the vehicle. They set off again, and Carvalho soon saw they had reached the end of the promenade and were coming to an area of big, dark warehouses. The van steered a path between crumbling fishing boats and oil drums, then turned into a cul-de-sac. It crossed a yard full of tubs of flowers and with a leafy vine clinging to a red-lead-painted iron frame, then pulled up inside a warehouse.

Carvalho parked his car at the corner of the cul-de-sac. He could see a faded sign hanging over the entrance to the yard: 'Ginés Larios Shipbuilders'. That seemed to refer to a previous use for the warehouse, because underneath another, more recent sign written in smaller letters announced its current function: 'Frozen Foods Company'. Carvalho could not hear the van engine any more, so he got out of his car, walked quickly up the short street and then slipped into the yard-cum-garden. His eyes were darting round so quickly his feet would hardly have been able to stop in time if he saw anything suspicious. Without quite knowing how, he found himself inside the warehouse, with his back pressed against the side of the van. He listened intently for any noise. As his eyes grew used to the gloom, he began to make out vague shapes strewn around the floor. At the far end of the building he saw a lit doorway. He edged his way over to it. Almost immediately beyond it rose an iron staircase; from up above came the sounds of family life and the clatter of plates.

'Why don't we eat outside under the vine?'

'Your mother might feel cold.'

By now Carvalho could make out enough to see everything inside the warehouse. He saw another door on the wall opposite the side of the van he had hidden behind. He went over to it, and when he pushed it open was surprised that it gave straight on to the beach and the sea, with the first stars in the night sky reflected on its waters. The warehouse building formed a corner at the edge of the beach. On the sand stood a rotting fishing smack and a fibreglass motorboat with an outboard engine protected by a rubber hood. Carvalho climbed on board both of them, feeling in every corner. When he was in the fibreglass boat he realised with a shock that the lighted window where he had heard the family talking looked directly on to the beach. He thought he saw someone looking out, and dived to the bottom of the boat. After waiting what seemed like centuries, he slowly raised his head. False alarm: there was nobody there.

He jumped down on to the sand and went back inside the

warehouse. Everything seemed quiet. He felt the bundles on the floor. Everything smelt of sea and fish. He opened the van door and slid in. The smell of fish was almost overpowering. He opened several tin boxes and saw they were full of packs of frozen fish. He felt round them, and when he was done jumped up into the driver's cabin. He opened a drawer in front of the passenger seat and pulled out a wad of invoices, dirty rags and a pair of sunglasses. The vehicle document showed an address that must be where he was now, and the name corresponded to what was written on the sign out front. All of a sudden, Carvalho heard a confusion of noise. He slipped into the back of the van again, and through the window watched as an entire family laden down with plates, pots and pans, chairs and a folding table made its way out to the yard. An elderly couple, two young men, Fat Nuria and an old woman in black gradually set out the things in the garden part, turning it into an improvised open-air restaurant.

'What have we got to eat, Mother?'

'Chitterlings.'

'Not chitterlings!'

'Your father likes them; he asks me for them every day. I'm not here to try to please everybody.'

She had a Murcian accent, swallowing all the ends of her words.

'So now you don't like chitterlings. You used to love them.'

The mother was talking. Carvalho tried to remember the taste of chitterlings. From his hiding place he could see a glazed pottery dish heaped full of them. He was so fascinated he forgot he was in hiding, and when he had to move was surprised that he had been crouching in the van for so long. He jumped out and edged back towards the beach. From here he could climb over a fence, go along another stretch of beach, over another wall and walk towards the lights that he supposed must mean it was a more inhabited area. But from there it might be difficult for him to get back to his car unseen. He preferred to wait for the family to finish dinner and go back inside before he tried to get out.

He lay flat on the sand alongside the motorboat. From where he was, the launch looked much bigger, and he had a mental picture of it cutting through the waves. All of a sudden something fell overboard. A human body. And as it fell on top of Carvalho, he could see its destroyed face. Carvalho was crushed beneath the weight of this imagined scene. Badalona was very near to both Vilasar and Caldetas. From this remote part of the beach it was easy to put to sea carrying any kind of cargo. Julio Chesma's dead body could have been taken out from here in the launch whose polished hull was up pressed against his nose.

The warehouse door swung open. A man came slowly down the sand, a cigarette between his lips. He walked straight between the motorboat and the fishing smack. He went to the water's edge, where the foam of the quiet night-time waves lapped at the shore. The man stood looking out to sea as though to fill his empty eyes with the tranquil dark. Then he lowered his hands to his midriff, and Carvalho soon saw a stream of urine descending silently, the sound obscured by the rumour of the waves. The man finished with a quick shake of the hand, and put the one-eyed snake back in his trousers. When he turned he was bound to see Carvalho. As he began to move, Carvalho tumbled into the boat. He collapsed to the bottom, and wriggled round until he could feel the reassuring crocodile-rough texture of his revolver butt. He ran his fingers over the cool metal. The man's footsteps were drawing closer as he walked back up the beach. He had reached the prow of the boat, then stepped between it and the fishing smack. Carvalho had rolled on to his back so that he could see if the man looked over the side of the boat at all.

But the footsteps carried on past him. Carvalho's fingers gradually relaxed on his gun butt. The tense pain in his chest eased, and he fell back into the soft curvature of the boat bottom. He heard the warehouse door being pulled shut. He felt the cool night breeze once more, this time on a forehead that had suddenly become pearled with sweat. He resigned himself to waiting in the same position as long as it might take.

Carvalho arrived home in Vallvidrera at four in the morning. He felt the kind of exhaustion that only hours lived twice over can produce. He made himself a roll with cold meat, lettuce and mayonnaise. He opened a can of Dutch beer and collapsed on the sofa without even the energy to light a fire. As he ate, his ability to think returned. There must be a link between Chesma and Señor Ramón, and another one between Señor Ramón and Fat Nuria's father. The triangle closed with the line leading Chesma to a sea that returned him with no face and with the mysterious tattoo as his only identifying mark.

That still meant he had no answer as to why Señor

Ramón had set him on the trail of the drowned man. Why ask him to identify someone he himself had killed? Either he did not know who he was, or he was interested in some way in bringing Carvalho in, having him investigate and reach some unknown conclusion. If this was all a settling of accounts between drug traffickers, why on earth did Señor Ramón need the services of a private detective?

And if this wasn't a settling of accounts between traffickers, what possible connection could there be between the owner of a harmless hairdressing salon and a man born to raise hell in hell?

This was as far as Carvalho got before he fell asleep. He was awakened at eleven the next morning by a desperate need to drink a cold orange juice. If there was something Carvalho was grateful to his body for, it was how in tune it was with its own needs. He had inherited his father's conviction that a person's body knows exactly what it needs and what it doesn't. Whenever he found he had a craving for sweet things, he thought: 'My body needs glucose.' Whenever he suddenly felt a passion for seafood, he said to himself: 'My body needs phosphorus.' And if it was lentils he was yearning for, he knew he was low on iron. He would never dare make a theory out of this physiological wisdom, but it had helped him survive thirty-seven years without any illnesses other than the occasional cold, which triggered a need for oranges and lemons.

It was very inconvenient to wake up longing for orange juice at a time of year when any sensible person knows not to buy them. He made do with some lemon, ice cubes and a little water. He needed to talk to Teresa Marsé and to have a swim. He drove down from Tibidabo into the city, hoping to be able to kill two birds with one stone. He burst into her boutique with the suggestion on his lips. She was in the back room pinning a dress on to a dummy, her mouth full of pins. She did not seem taken aback when Carvalho suddenly appeared and asked her to drop everything and go for a swim with him. She took so long to reply that Carvalho began to doubt whether she would come and so in turn adopted a cooler, more sceptical attitude. His disgruntled voice seemed to be coming out of his boots by the time she was able to mumble through her mouthful of sadistic pins:

'Wait a minute. I'll be with you right away and we can go.'

Carvalho appreciated the way she was as good as her word. Charo would have taken twenty times as long, always finding new things to do before she could fulfil that 'right away'. But Teresa was ready in no time, and the only surprise she gave Carvalho was when she took off her blonde Angela Davis wig. Her own hair was an attractive auburn. She combed it through with a couple of expert strokes, then turned to Carvalho, all set for adventure. Stripped of the caricature of curls, Teresa once more became a daughter of the upper middle classes, her features sculptured by healthy eating and proper hygiene. She had the relaxed, self-confident look of a high-wire acrobat who knows they are working with a safety net. Charo by contrast had never had a safety net, and occasionally Carvalho caught the cruel, trapped look on her face of someone who would kill to defend herself, or was frightened of a fall. Working-class faces seem to be as stiff as caryatids: either laughter or tears. Teresa's face conveyed a sense of calm that made sense to anyone who knew they could survive anywhere and at any time.

Teresa was carrying a beach bag in one hand, and pulled Pepe along with the other. They decided to take his car.

'Which beach should we go to? There's always wind at Castelldefels and Garraf.'

'Let's head north. What about Caldetas?'

Teresa had suggested it without Carvalho even having to intervene. They drove in silence because she seemed interested only in listening to the radio or a cassette. Whenever a song she liked came on the radio, she leaned back in her seat, closed her eyes and folded her arms behind her head. This gave Carvalho the chance to study the flat contours of her body, more evident under her tunic. But what he liked about Teresa was her attitude, a capacity for lovemaking that was obvious from the nonchalant way she played the game, a theatrical *savoir faire* which she would doubtless know how to adapt to any situation.

'We're there.'

She seemed to wake up. Without hesitation, she lifted her tunic over her head and sat there in her bikini. Carvalho looked her body up and down appreciatively. The second time he was moving up from her ankles, her eyes met his. She was smiling.

'*Pas mal*?'

'*Pas mal.*'

She burst out laughing, touched him on the arm and for a split second leant her cheek on his shoulder. The car headed down towards the centre of Caldetas, aiming for the passageway under the railway line. The rows of villas looked as if they came straight out of a history of modern architecture in Catalonia, and gave the impression that the resort offered more as a living museum than as somewhere for a swim. The sight of all the turn-of-the-century houses, many of them run-down and dark, led Carvalho to think that when they reached the beach they would stumble on a scene of belle époque bathers sitting under parasols in their long bathing costumes, engaged in polite conversation with remarks such as:

'What a beautiful morning it is.'

But when they got to the beach and lay down with their backs to the town, Caldetas was just like any other Costa Brava beach, with unremarkable sand full of people trying to get away from the polluted beaches of Barcelona. Whereas to the south of the city you could find Charo's friends busy tanning their merchandise and swarthy Romeos in the briefest of swimwear, the northern beaches like this one attracted middle-class women who could not get enough of the sun, surrounded by children who all of a sudden would rush off shouting 'Papa! Papa!' when the head of the family appeared, having successfully made his escape from his arduous duties back in the city.

Teresa plunged into the sea with the ease of someone who has the habit of swimming and knows she can do a perfect breaststroke. Carvalho lay on the sand with his hands behind his head. He watched as Teresa ploughed up and down, then headed back towards the shore in a perfect straight line. She ran up the beach shaking herself to get rid of the water streaming down her, then flung herself next to Carvalho on the towel waiting for her on the sand like a rectangular parking space.

Carvalho did not like lying in the sun like a lizard, but Teresa showed that her body thermostat was the same as that of all other women, cold-blooded creatures who need the sun and are capable of soaking up its rays with the beatific expression of someone taking communion, or even the ecstatic look of a mystic surrendering to the godhead. Teresa's face beamed ecstatically. It was more than Carvalho could bear, so he decided to go for a swim, even though he had no great wish to. He realised his nose was blocked, and immediately linked it to having spent most of the previous night out in the cold air, as well as his craving for orange juice when he had woken up that morning. Despite this, he dived in and swam for five minutes so that he could somehow identify with Teresa and flop down beside her again with a sense of shared pleasure.

'I'm hungry,' she said, and for once did not add the feared: 'Let's go and eat any old thing'. 'We could have lunch in a restaurant. There must be some good ones here. When I used to spend the summer in Caldetas with my parents we sometimes went to one on the promenade. I don't know if it's still there. Or we could have sausages and beer. That would save time, and I could show you our house.'

Carvalho felt something flutter inside his chest. To avoid stumbling over the words, he said nothing. They dried themselves and went back to his car. Carvalho kept guard outside while she got changed. She put her tunic on and took off her wet bikini. Then she carefully dried between her legs. Carvalho wrapped his towel round his waist, let his trunks fall to the ground, and sat inside the car. He dressed quickly, trying to avoid anyone passing by and catching him unawares.

'We could walk. It's right here. Then we could pick up the car to go to the house.'

They walked hand in hand up to the promenade. The sausage stall was surrounded by a crowd of bathers and others who had returned to more conventional attire, all of them attracted by the smell of sausages on the grill.

Carvalho was pleased to see that the choice was not limited to the tyranny of the frankfurter, but that there were also smoked sausages cooking. He was afraid Teresa might submit their stomachs to the tyranny of the frankfurter, so he quickly suggested:

'Why don't we have some of the smoked sausages?'

'I've never tried them. Are they the white ones over there?'

'No, but the white ones are good as well. We could eat one smoked sausage and one of the white ones if you like.'

'No frankfurters?'

It seemed as though Teresa's stomach would be lost without them, so Carvalho relented:

'All right, have a frankfurter, but try a smoked sausage as well.'

Carvalho smeared his sausages with ketchup. Teresa went for the tried-and-tested mustard. The draught beer was surprisingly good, and Pepe was taken aback to find that after the smoked sausage and a frankfurter he still had room for a hot dog with mustard.

'It was excellent. There's only one place in Barcelona that does such good sausages.'

'Which place is that?'

Carvalho gave her the details and how to get there. Teresa looked interested and amused. Then they walked back to the car and drove until they came to the iron gates at the entrance to her family villa. She got out to undo the padlock. She opened the gates wide, and Carvalho found himself confronted by a gravel drive that looped round two sides of a planted border taken over by several dwarf palm trees. He turned down the right-hand side and drove slowly past untended hedges and straggly oleander bushes that pushed weakly against the windshield. Behind the bushes were cement walls encrusted with pieces of coloured tile, and there were more pots in a similar style that boasted huge tangles of geraniums. The drive ended in front of the main entrance to the house. The huge villa built in almost purple stone was topped off by ornate pointed turrets decorated with more brightly coloured shards of glass tile.

Mosaic steps led up to a triple-arched door excavated in the mass of purplish sandstone, which glittered with thousand of crystals and more bits of tile set in the walls like precious stones. Teresa came panting up behind Carvalho.

'Why didn't you wait for me?'

She opened the middle arch of the door and Carvalho found himself in a grand hallway. The dampness inside was almost solid, pierced here and there like a Gruyère cheese by the coloured rays of sunlight streaming in through the cracked stained-glass windows. They showed scenes from the arts and crafts of medieval and Renaissance Catalonia. neo-Gothic columns were prominent in the high walls, interrupted every so often by stucco bas-reliefs painted in what must once have been a shiny brown. At the start of the coffee-coloured marble balustrade a faded plaster San Jorge was raising his lance above the head of a twisting, sullen-looking lizard-cum-dragon. Set high in the wall at the far end of the hall was a small rose window, where the Catalan flag concentrated the gaze in an exaltation of the power and the glory of a bourgeoisie in its creative and productive prime.

'I can't possibly show you all of it. There are some rooms I haven't seen since I was a child. They're locked anyway. When we all came for our holidays we used to have four maids.'

To one side of the staircase was the library. It was lined with wooden bookshelves, while the ceiling was made of wooden stalactites hanging down like a fairy-tale forest. Every inch of the walls was crammed with books. They went into the living room next door, where lumpy armchairs seemed to be waiting for a fire to miraculously spring up in the grey granite hearth, meant to be a faithful copy of the ones in the ancient farmhouses of the Catalan countryside. Carvalho stooped to examine the chimney: no sign of any inferior wood ever being burned there in the past five hundred years at least, he decided indignantly. From the living room they passed into the dining room, as majestic as the boardroom of an English bank, decorated according to the precepts of William Morris, although its neo-Gothic splendour seemed at odds with the four Sunyer paintings hanging from the walls. Peasant scenes for the posh, thought Carvalho. A narrow passageway connected the dining room to the kitchens, which still had the rancid smell of age-old stew. The kitchen was badly laid out, with sets of battered saucepans hanging from the walls and coke-burning stoves with doors that had buckled from the heat.

Another passageway led out of the other side of the kitchen. Halfway along it, a set of steps went down to the wine cellar. At the end of the corridor, they were back in the entrance hall.

'The bedrooms are upstairs.'

Teresa took the stairs two at a time. Carvalho followed in her wake, and they soon arrived at the embossed wooden doors of the main bedroom. A high Gothic-looking four-poster bed. A neoclassical dressing table with a tilting mirror. A mahogany chest of drawers with flowery scrolls and a marble top with blackened cracks on it. At first, Carvalho did not notice the painting above the chest of drawers facing the bed. It was only when Teresa took him by the hand and pulled him over to the wooden platform around the four-poster that he paid it any real attention. As he fell on to the bed and began to get serious with Teresa he looked round the room one last time and was struck by the painting's livid, almost phosphorescent colours. It was an example of the classic moral painting that the pious Catalan bourgeoisie hung in their bedrooms to help them avoid the temptation of wanting more contact than the slit in their wife's nightgown or even, God forbid! the acting out of something they had only heard of in a smutty joke. The painting represented the biblical scene of Lucifer's revolt. The fallen angel appeared in the bottom right-hand corner of the canvas, about to begin his descent down a mysterious staircase in order to escape the deadly threat of the archangel Michael's broadsword.

'Born to raise hell in hell,' thought Carvalho, just as he sensed Teresa's warm skin calling out to him and felt her hand wriggling like a cool dove beneath his shirt.

'We should be getting back. You have to pick up your boy.'

'His father's collecting him today. It's his granny's birthday and he's going there for tea.'

She said the word 'granny' with heavy sarcasm. Carvalho had curled up against her body under a yellowing sheet. From that position all he could see was the silk pouch of the four-poster canopy above his head or the painting of Lucifer, neatly framed in between the two posts at the foot of the bed.

'Did Julio spend many hours in this bed?'

'Quite a few. Why?'

'Look.'

Teresa raised her body and turned to gaze at the picture.

'I didn't remember that was there,' she said, lying down again a bit farther away from Carvalho. 'Do you always spend your time in bed talking about people who have been there before you?'

'We don't have that much in common to talk about.'

'If that's how you feel, ask away. I'm an open book.'

'Did he talk to you about his tattoo?'

MANUEL VÁZQUEZ MONTALBÁN |||

'When I saw it I couldn't stop laughing. I asked him to get rid of it. He wouldn't hear of such a thing.'

'You met when he came back from Holland two years ago. How long did your relationship last?'

'Not long, four or five months. After that we saw each other occasionally, until a few months ago.'

'Did he ask you for the key often?'

'At first, yes. Then I told him to get copies cut and have done with it.'

'Did you never visit here at the same time?'

'Yes. Once. I didn't want to tell you the other night because you frightened me. It was seven or eight months ago. In January, I think. I came with a member of the Persian royal family. Yes, that's right. A third cousin of the shah. He wrote to me because he has a store selling hippy stuff. I could tell someone was here because the garden gate was open. But there are lots of bedrooms in the house. I consulted his royal highness, and although at first he was put out, he agreed anyway. We came in and went to another room at the far end of this floor. I was dying of curiosity, so I sneaked back here. I opened the door as quietly as I could. Julio was on the bed, and looked as though he was fast asleep. Next to him lay an older woman. Well, not that old really: she must have been around forty. She wasn't asleep. She seemed to be staring out of the window. The shutters were slightly open and she was staring at the sky.'

'Did Julio ever mention her?'

'No.'

'Can you describe her?'

'I only saw a sheet and above it a dark-haired woman, a

big face, eyes and nose and so on... her body seemed to fill the sheet quite well.'

Queta's buxom charms would have fitted the scene far better than Teresa's well-toned but scrawny body. What Carvalho found harder to imagine was the feelings a hairdresser from District Five in Barcelona might have in this sanctuary dedicated to the leisure of a social class totally alien to her. All at once Carvalho was transported back to the 1940s, his mind opening in the same miraculous way as had happened when many of the streets of District Five had been cleared to make room for the Plaza Padró. He remembered songs on the radio drifting through the interior courtyards above the background sounds of sewing-machines or plates clinking in earthernware washing-up bowls. Above all he remembered a song sung by all the women who were then the same age as Queta was now:

He arrived on a boat with a foreign name
She met him in the port at nightfall

A love song for a stranger 'as bold and blond as beer', with 'a heart tattooed on his chest'. For the first time in his life Julio had met a woman who was mentally inferior to him. Someone who did not offer him culture or new experiences, but simply wanted the companionship and solidarity he could give, plus some personal enrichment and the mystery of youth and far-off lands that had been dead and buried long ago for Señor Ramón. To her, that tattoo had a meaning, it was the meaning of her life. It was like a secret whispered in that four-poster bed that was alien to both of them, a secret into which, on his long journey from poverty to nothingness, the man she was with had poured all his lifetime's rage: 'Born to raise hell in hell'. A motto that had not been put there for a theatrical widow in Rotterdam who wanted to save her working-class heroes through culture, nor for the woodpecker Teresa Marsé, pecking away in all sorts of trees, nor for Frenchy or any other love for hire. Carvalho felt an urgent need to wipe away the images he could see in his mind's eye, to jump out of bed and run with burning sword in hand to give the whole thing its *coup de grâce*.

He sat up like a man on the run.

'Is that it? Is the afternoon over for you?'

'Yes.'

'Do you always buy a single ticket?'

'That depends on who I'm travelling with.'

'Thanks a lot.'

When he saw the twinkle of amusement in Teresa's eye Carvalho wondered whether he should stay where he was and make sure she was not disappointed. Yet he suddenly realised he was not the slightest bit interested in this skinny woman who would probably chat about the experience with her husband or with the group of piranha friends she met in the smart cafés of Calle Tuset.

'I calculated my time to fit in with yours. I thought you had to go and fetch your son at the usual time, so I made an appointment then as well.'

This seemed to satisfy Teresa. She turned her back on Carvalho to get dressed. She spoke facing away from him.

'You're a cop, aren't you?'

'Why do you say that?'

'I could tell from the start. You ask questions like a cop.'

'Actually I'm not.'

'So why are you so interested in Julio?'

'I was hired. I'm a private detective.'

Teresa guffawed. She laughed so much she collapsed on the bed half-dressed. When the laughter subsided she had to wipe away the tears.

'So who have I been sleeping with: Hercule Poirot, Inspector Maigret or Philip Marlowe?'

'If you prefer you can say you slept with Lemmy Caution or James Bond.'

'I don't like James Bond.'

'You choose, then. I've given you the experience of your lifetime.'

'I have to tell you that the shah's cousin was more exciting, and he didn't have to rush off. A real gentleman, the sort you remember for a long time.'

'You already have a husband for that kind of thing.'

The escape from the tomb of a house, the return to the car and the journey back to Barcelona all took place in silence. Teresa did not even switch the radio on. As Carvalho pulled up outside her boutique, he warned her:

'Think up a good alibi for the first fortnight in July. Try to remember everything you did. A water-tight alibi that isn't too complicated.'

'Why?'

'It's very likely that Julio Chesma was killed then, either in your villa at Caldetas or because of someone he used to meet there. The police could discover that at any moment.'

'Was it linked to drugs?'

'That's what I thought at first. But now I don't think so. Come up with an alibi.'

Teresa stared hard at him, as if trying to discover an ulterior motive.

'Am I supposed to thank you?'

'Don't bother. Just remember what I said, and if the police question you, don't so much as mention my name.'

Teresa got out of the car. From the boutique doorway she cast him one last dubious glance.

All Charo said was:
'It's the worst possible time.'
'I'll leave right away.'
'I don't hear from you in days, then you appear at the very worst moment.'
'Is your Andalusian friend there?'
'No.'
'What does her hair look like?'
'How's it supposed to look? It's normal.'
'I'll pay her for a hairdo and invite you both to dinner one of these days if she goes to Queta's again.'
'But she only went two days ago.'
'Tell her to mess up her hair.'
Carvalho wrote something on a piece of paper and put it in a small envelope.
'Here. Give it to your friend. Tell her to go and get her hair done tomorrow, and when she has the chance, to slip this to Queta without anyone else seeing.'
'Now what? Goodbye and good luck?'
'It's your peak time. I don't think you want me to meet your clients.'
'My clients and you can both take a walk.'

Charo stormed out of her living room and rushed into the kitchen, slamming the door behind her. Carvalho could hear her shouting, as though she were arguing with herself. They're all such cretins! And you, you're an idiot! Such an idiot!

To frustrate two women in one day was too much even for Carvalho. He left the apartment, but then waited out on the landing for Charo's inevitable attempt to put things right. When she opened her front door and poked her head out, her face was streaked with tears. Her voice was unsteady:

'Are you going to leave just like that?'

'You've got a busy day.'

'That doesn't mean you can just vanish.'

'I've got a lot of work tomorrow. Try to keep the evening free. We could go out somewhere.'

'Will you come and fetch me?'

'OK. At nine.'

He walked out to the Rambla and headed down towards the port. When he reached Santa Mónica church he left the central reservation, crossed the pavement on the right-hand side, and slipped into the narrow street on the left of the church. He went into El Pastis bar and ordered an absinthe. The bar owner had the visual memory of an elephant.

'Haven't seen you in a long time.'

Carvalho smiled at her, trying to convey the impression that he too was the victim of fate that rules over all encounters.

'But everyone comes back in the end. Look at that lot over there.'

A group of youngsters was sitting with glasses of pastis. Their faces were flushed, and it was obvious they all had the ultimate quip on the tip of their tongue. One of them suggested they all sang the 'Internationale', while another tried to improvise a speech in honour of thirty-three years of peace in Spain.

'They'll all be back in a few years, you'll see. When they're grown up and respectable. Like this gentleman, this eminence.'

She pointed to a man farther down the bar. He was in his thirties and was staring intently at a candle on the counter. He lifted himself on his elbows and stared at Carvalho in an arrogant, challenging way.

'See him there? I knew him when he was a student, and now look at him, world famous he is.'

'Good luck to him.'

The world-famous eminence studied Carvalho through bleary eyes, ready to explode if he thought the detective was undermining him in any way.

'He's a university professor.'

The drunken guy looked like a Bourbon prince on his uppers. He was tall and with the kind of features usually described in neoclassical terms as harmonious. The eminent prince started to harangue Carvalho in a language that sounded like Arabic. The bar owner nodded enthusiastically, and pointed at him again.

'Are you a professor of Arabic?'

'No, of Spanish history. But what can one know about the history of Spain if one doesn't speak Arabic?'

'You're probably right.'

'Menéndez Pinal got it all wrong. Do you know who he was?'

'The name rings a bell.'

'The man who invented El Cid. An anti-Arab racist. Here, have a pastis. On me.'

The eminent prince started to sing an Arab melody which bit by bit turned into a fandango. He had lifted the lapels of his jacket, and folded them in so that it looked as though he were wearing a dancer's waistcoat. He stared down at his toes, and began an unsteady tap dance. Carvalho set down the money for his pastis and made to leave, but felt the professor's hand on his shoulder.

'Why did you pay? I said I would.'

'I pay for my own drinks.'

'Not when I offer you one.'

With that, the professor swept the money Carvalho had left on the counter on to the floor. The bar owner came out from behind the counter, picked it up and handed it to Carvalho, winking at him. Pepe shrugged, took the money and went out into the street. He had almost reached the Rambla when he heard the sound of rapid footsteps behind his back, almost level with him. He turned and found himself face to face with the professor.

'Did you know that all the studies of Spanish place names are wrong? Wrong? No, that's not the word. Stolen! They've been stolen, in order to hide their true identity from everyone! They want us to forget our Arab roots!'

They were walking past heaps of rubble on the pavement outside Santa Mónica church. Overcome by a sudden impulse, Carvalho pushed the professor hard. He stumbled and fell on his side on to a pile of dirt. Carvalho ran off as quickly as he could. It was only when he was by the sentry boxes in front of the navy headquarters that he slowed to walking pace again. He thought he could hear the professor shouting close behind him, so as soon as he was beyond the lit zone of the headquarters he broke into a run once more, and turned into the dark, narrow streets of the Chinese quarter. He had left his car in a car park on Calle Barbará. He was worried that he had not managed to shake the drunken professor off, and in fact met up with him again outside the Cádiz dance hall. The other man had guessed which way he would go and had got ahead of him. He was standing there with legs wide apart, his fists in the air as though ready to go fifteen rounds with him.

'Come and get it, you little fucker. See how you get on with Muhammad Ali.'

There was no one else about. The consumptive, filthy street lights scarcely managed to bring a vague glow to the darkened street. Carvalho felt in his pocket and pulled out his switchblade. He let his opponent lunge at him, then slashed the air only an inch from the professor's nose. The eminent prince backed off, and stared at Carvalho in bewilderment.

'Oho, a knife fighter, are we?'

But he did not come forward again. Full of rage, Carvalho charged, knife at the ready. The other man tried to dodge him, but fell flat on his back on the ground. Carvalho kicked him mercilessly. He was trying to get at his face, but the professor lifted his arms to protect himself.

'Hey, what's going on there?' Two whores emerged

from the Cádiz. It looked as if one of them was about to call the police, so Carvalho quickly put away his knife and calmly walked off. He could feel a warm glow in his chest, as if he had drunk a glass of fine French brandy or Black Label whisky.

Carvalho's note read: 'I'd like to talk to you about Julio. Just the two of us. Meet me at four in the Luna bar, on the corner of the Rambla and Plaza Catalunya'. At five to four he saw Queta crossing the Rambla. She was wearing a loose-fitting sleeveless dress with sandals, and carried a red bag. Carvalho acknowledged that she was a woman worth looking at. The erotic effect of her still-fresh body was enhanced by the suffering, anxious look on her face. She found Carvalho and came and stood in front of his table. He got up and pointed her to a metal chair. She wanted nothing, but he forced her to accept a coffee. She sat down defensively, ready to double her usual efforts to hide her vulnerability.

'Let's have our drinks then get in my car. It's always better to be sure our talk stays private.'

'I've no idea what you and I have to talk about. I don't know what you want. I don't know what your note meant.'

'Why did you come, then?'

She had no answer. Her defences were crumbling. She could not even look Carvalho in the face.

'Look. I know all about your relations with Julio Chesma. Your husband hired me to discover the identity of a drowned man washed up on the beach at Vilasar a few weeks ago. His face had been devoured by fish, but he had a tattoo with a motto on his back.'

Carvalho did not go on. Queta was sobbing into a handkerchief; she was on the verge of collapsing into complete hysteria. Carvalho hurriedly took out some money, paid the bill and led her out. He almost dragged her to the car park opposite the Coliseum cinema. The car park attendant looked at the sobbing woman with alarm. Carvalho shrugged as if to show how impossible it was for men to fathom the absurd psychology of women.

He came out on to Gran Vía and headed for the coastal motorway. Queta seemed to have got over the shock. Her breathing was back to normal, and she seemed to be enjoying looking out at the countryside. When they reached Masnou and the sea appeared, shimmering in the late afternoon sunlight, she turned nervously to Carvalho.

'Where are you taking me?'

'To Caldetas.'

'I don't want to go there!'

'Perhaps it won't be necessary.'

'I don't want to go! I'll jump out of the car! You have no right to kidnap me like this!'

'Perhaps it won't be necessary. I know almost everything that happened. I just need to fill in a few details.'

Queta was staring at the road as though with each passing kilometre she was losing something more.

'How did you meet Julio?'

'Which Julio?'

'The one in my note. I wrote his name there, and you knew who I meant.'

'I only found out he was called Julio when you told Ramón.'

'How did you meet him?'

'What does it matter? What do you care? Please. I don't want to go back to that place. Please.'

'We could drive around until you've told me what I want to know.'

'I met him in a cinema. Ramón doesn't like films, so sometimes I go to local ones in the early evenings when there aren't many clients left.'

'Was this a long time ago?'

'A little more than a year. Maybe a year and a half. I don't know why I was such a fool. Now God has punished us. All of us.'

'What did he say his name was?'

'Alejandro.'

'Did you start going to the Caldetas villa right from the beginning?'

'No, at first he took me to places he knew.'

'What kind of places?'

'That kind of place.'

'Motels?'

She did not answer. She was staring down into her lap.

'Weren't you surprised he didn't take you back to where he lived?'

'He said he had a landlady. Then we started going to the villa. He said it belonged to some cousins of his.'

'Did he look like the sort of person who would have cousins owning a place like that?'

'He was very classy. Very well educated. Very knowledgeable.'

'Did your husband know about it?'

'No.'

'But in the end he found out.'

'No.'

'So why did he ask me to identify a body when he already knew perfectly well who it was?'

'He didn't know his real name.'

'Which means you admit he knew the existence of your little friend.'

'I didn't say that.'

Carvalho leaned over towards her and shouted:

'Don't be so stupid! The cops wouldn't be as polite as I am, and then you'd sing like a canary in ten seconds flat.'

'Don't shout at me. Who are you to shout at me? Let me out.'

'When did your husband find out?'

'I don't know.'

'I want to know how he died.'

'He drowned.'

'No, he didn't drown. Or if he did, your husband was watching. The newspapers made no link between the drowned man and the police raids, but your husband linked the two immediately.'

'You know what our neighbourhood is like. There are lots of informers. Not all of Ramón's business deals are above board. Why fool ourselves? He has connections.'

'Obviously not good enough ones if he has to hire me to discover or confirm the identity of a drowned man. Don't try to pull the wool over my eyes, or I'll stop at the first police station.'

'So what? So I had a friend. Or a lover, if you prefer. Ramón already knows that, so what could happen to me?'

'Not every lover appears drowned in such mysterious circumstances and with all that happened afterwards. Let me complete the story. Your husband finds out. He kills your lover. Throws him into the sea. Then he hears that the cops are after a gang of drug traffickers who might be connected to the dead man. It all gets more complicated than he thought, and he's in the middle of it. He hires me to see if there is any other possible link besides drugs. By the time I get back from Holland, everything has gone perfectly for your Ramón. The cops are convinced the death is all about drugs, and neither of you two has been brought into it. He acted too hastily by getting me involved, so he wanted to wrap everything up once and for all. Job done and paid for. But that wasn't the end of it: by now, I was too interested in the case.'

'Why? What do you want?'

'More money. That could be an explanation. Or perhaps I simply want to close the case to my own satisfaction. I don't like mysteries: that's why I've chosen a trade that tries to unpick them.'

'I won't say that Ramón killed Julio.'

'But he did. It must have been in the villa. The owner saw traces of blood there.' Queta buried her face in her hands. 'And he couldn't have done it alone. How could he have tackled a man as brave and blond as beer?'

Queta looked at him in complete bewilderment.

'It was probably the Larios family who gave him a hand. The father, or the two brothers. They owe him lots of favours. For a start, the fact that he gave Fat Nuria a job. Am I right?'

By now Queta was staring at him with something approaching admiration.

'Was it them?'

She stared out again at the highway speeding past.

'And you were there too. They caught you at it, didn't they?'

Queta was in tears.

'The fool thought he was born to raise hell in hell, and he died because he was fucking someone else's wife. Did you look away while they finished him off?'

By now she was hysterical, beating her hands against the side window.

'I want to go! Let me out of here!'

Carvalho thumped her on the back so hard it took her breath away.

'I'll take you home now. Tell your husband about our little chat and tell him we didn't make it to the Caldetas villa. He needn't worry about me blabbing to the police. But tomorrow I'm coming to the salon, and I want to talk to him. I've put a lot of effort into this and I've found out so much I reckon I haven't been paid enough. Especially if I don't like what he has to say to me.'

Queta watched him come into the salon without moving a muscle. As usual, Fat Nuria tried to get in front of him and by the time he had climbed the stairs she was already on guard outside Señor Ramón's office. The old man waited for Carvalho to sit down, then signalled for her to leave. When he was sure it was just the two of them, he opened a drawer, pulled out an envelope and threw it across the desk. It fell into Carvalho's lap. He opened it slowly. Counted the money inside. A hundred thousand pesetas.

'Take them and get out of here.'

Carvalho put the money back in the envelope, then flung it in Señor Ramón's face.

'I haven't decided yet whether I want to be paid off or not.'

'What do you want then? I'm sure Queta has told you everything.'

'In fact, it was me who told your wife everything, and she didn't deny it.'

'What exactly did you tell her?'

'You discover your wife has a lover. You turn up at

their hiding place with some friends. You kill him. You take the body in a frozen-foods delivery van to the Larios family warehouse in Badalona. You stow the body in a motorboat. Put swimming trunks on him. Then take him out to sea and throw him overboard. But it turns out he's a dangerous corpse. He weighs about the same as a good shipment of drugs. You start getting alarming news. You see you might be linked to the death, either by the cops, or by the dead man's friends. You don't even know his real name. The police are snooping around, making enquiries. You hire me to find out who he was because that way I'll come to the case pure as driven snow and will return to you with fresh, untainted information. Bad luck for you that I become interested in the victim. It doesn't always happen. I used to love literature, Señor Ramón. Now I only like real-life literature, and our friend was what you might call a wasted literary hero. So I followed the leads I had, and lo and behold I stumble across the woman in the song, the real woman in the song.'

'What song are you talking about?'

'That's my business. The facts are as I've told you. By the time I got back from Holland you knew the police investigation was aimed exclusively at the drug connection. That has nothing to do with you. You were in the clear, my friend, and didn't need me any longer.'

'Take the hundred thousand and get out.'

'Why did you kill him?'

'Don't you think I had a motive?'

'You don't seem like a man governed by passion. In fact, you killed him in cold blood, and had help.'

'Are you so sure I killed him?'

'Who else could it have been?'

'That woman is a real piece of shit.'

Señor Ramón had become agitated. His face was so flushed with anger that his pale freckles had vanished completely. He got to his feet and was trembling with fury.

'She changed my whole life. I left everything for her. Do you think I was born to run a pathetic little business like this? That woman was the manicurist of my real wife. Fifteen years ago I had style and the strength and the nerve to crush you and that layabout at the same time. I left everything for her, and it was all going well until he appeared. She's like a jelly: no backbone. He picked her up off the street and she didn't even think of all I'd sacrificed for her, of everything I had lost.'

Suddenly, as though all his rage and strength had suddenly deserted him, he collapsed back into his chair.

'I'm old enough now to live a peaceful existence. My wife, the real one, is enjoying a harmonious old age, surrounded by my children and grandchildren. And at my age I need some attention, I need looking after every day. It's a time when the most important thing to a man is harmony.'

His fingers were moving through the air as though playing a piano.

'I probably wouldn't have done anything if I hadn't seen them with my own eyes. I went there with some friends to give him a good hiding, and to scare her. She really is a heap of shit, let me tell you. As soon as she saw us come in she started dragging herself across the floor, trying to kiss my hands. She was naked, stark naked! He means nothing to me, Ramón! You're my life! I owe everything to you! While she was pleading with me like that, the others were beating him up in the background, until he lost consciousness.'

He leaned back in his swivel chair. Now the look he gave Carvalho was the smile of someone about to reveal a secret.

'Do you want to know what happened then?'

He did not wait for Carvalho to reply.

'She was trying to cling to me. She couldn't have cared less what had happened to him. Ramón, my life! He doesn't mean a thing to me, I swear! You're the only one who matters!'

Ramón was gazing at Carvalho like a card-sharp sure of his hand.

'All I did was give her the small bronze statue from the chest of drawers.'

Carvalho blinked. He could feel his eyeballs filling with blood.

'All I did was hand it to her. She knew what she had to do with it.'

Carvalho looked away from Señor Ramón's face, desperately searching for some fixed point in the room to hold on to.

'She obliterated his face. She must have hit him a hundred times with the statue. When we dragged her off him there wasn't a single recognisable feature left.'

Carvalho felt tired. He could tell by the way he was grateful for the solid seat beneath him, and the fact that all of a sudden the sound of Señor Ramón's voice sounded almost pleasant.

'I did all the rest to protect her. I hired you, as you said, because I was worried about how important the case seemed to have become. Look at these.'

He rummaged in the drawer again and brought out two airline tickets.

'If you had worried me with what you found out, or if the police had come here asking questions, I would have flown far away. With her. Just the two of us.'

He pointed to Queta's name on one of the tickets.

'Two wrongs don't make a right, Señor Carvalho. There's no denying that. But I, or rather we, still have hope.'

He pointed to the envelope full of money, urging Carvalho to take it.

'If all this stays between the two of us, I'll double the amount.'

Carvalho knew the moment had come for him to exit stage right. But he still felt so weary he would have preferred Señor Ramón to be the one to go. He waited in vain, hoping against hope that he would fall asleep until everyone had left the salon and he could finally go home. He did not even hear the old man's final words, telling him the sordid details of how it all ended. Carvalho forced himself up. He turned his back on Señor Ramón and went down the stairs. He crossed the hairdressing salon like someone walking through an empty tunnel. He stood paralysed in the centre of the Rambla until he realised where he was, then headed south until almost without knowing it he reached the foot of the steps by the oily waters of the Las Golodrinas landing-stage. He bought a ticket and stepped on board the ferry that crossed the port to the breakwater. He walked along the top of it, peering at the languid old fishermen lounging in various states of undress in the sun's oppressive heat. Somehow it all seemed very familiar to him. He gradually recalled a scene from his schooldays: the wharf where the *musclaires* fished from their huts on stilts, while streams of soggy condoms floated past like sins. One sin for each condom.

'Do they throw them off ships?' a more innocent schoolmate asked.

'They come out of the drains.'

The smell of frying tomatoes and onions made life more bearable once more. It was coming from a shack at the bottom of some cement steps built in the wall of the breakwater. He could see steaming pots of mussels. It was high time to eat and comfort his complaining stomach.

Charo told him the news over the phone. Nothing for it but to buy a paper. He made a special trip down to the printer's in Vallvidrera to get the first evening edition. In *Tele/eXprés*, Fernando Casado reported the discovery with a lurid account of all that had happened. The body of Don Ramón Freixas had been found in a business he owned, a hairdressing salon in District Five. When two sisters who worked in the salon had arrived that morning they found the front door open. Don Ramón had a pair of scissors sticking out of his neck. The police were looking for one Enriqueta Sánchez Cámara, the victim's common-law wife ever since he had left his family some years earlier.

Carvalho wandered along a path on the hillside, letting his legs choose a route in among pine trees and brambles, under a fierce sun that brought out the smell of resin and vegetation. All of a sudden he remembered how the song ended:

Sailor, sit down and tell me
The news I am longing to hear
Remember how tall and proud he was
As bold and blond as beer...

Look, this is the name of the stranger
Tattooed right here on my skin
Sailor, if your ships ever cross
Say that I'm dying for him.

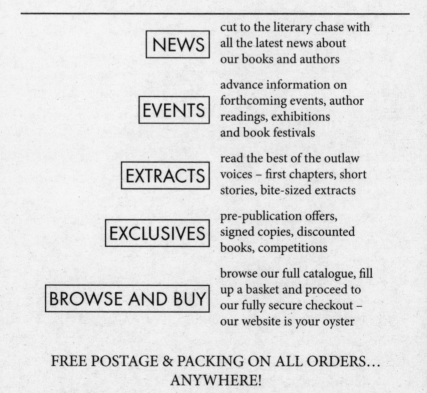